The Petrine Promise

a Vatican conspiracy thriller

REGNUM DEI

The Petrine Promise

a Vatican conspiracy thriller

by

Dr. R. Celestine

REGNUM DEI

THE PETRINE PROMISE

a Vatican conspiracy thriller

The REGNUM DEI logo design belongs to the publisher.

Canva book cover design

Manufactured in the United States of America

ISBN 9798316883080

For more information on upcoming book releases, related products and services and special discounts for bulk purchases, please contact:

info@midheavens.org

WWW.MIDHEAVENS.ORG

To my loving husband

RUDOLPH CELESTINE

Table of Contents

PROLOGUE: Jerusalem, 33AD

THE COMMISSION

The evening air hung heavy in the upper room. Jesus looked at each of His disciples in turn, His gaze lingering longest on those He had chosen to record His teachings.

"I have told you many times", He said quietly, "you must bear witness because you have been with me from the beginning".

John, the youngest, leaned forward. "Master, how will we know our writings have been true to Your teachings?"

"The Father Himself will give you the words", Jesus answered. "Just as He gave words to Moses, He will guide your testimonies". His expression grew serious. "But take heed- there will be those who try to change what you write, who will add their own teachings to yours. Beware- know that not all who shout 'Lord, Lord' will be pure of heart. Not all who prophesy on My behalf or cast out devils on My behalf or even do wonderful things on My behalf- are truly

1

with Me. I have warned you before- you must remain as wise as serpents and as harmless as doves".

Matthew, the former tax collector, had already begun taking notes, as was his custom. "Then how will future generations know which writings are true?"

"By their fruits, they shall know them". Jesus stood, moving to the window that overlooked Jerusalem. In the distance, the lights from oil lamps flickered in the high priest's palace. "There are those, even now, who fear the message of justice and accountability that I have taught you. They will not rest until they have created their own version of My teachings".

"Then we must protect the truth", Peter declared.

"Yes". Jesus turned back to them. "What you write will be preserved, though many will try to destroy it or bury it beneath other teachings. But in the last days, when the world most needs My message, what *you* have written will be rediscovered".

He touched the scrolls where Matthew had been writing his notes. "Your testimonies and those of your fellow Apostles who share in this task will be enough. Let no one add to them or take away from them".

In the streets below, torches appeared, moving towards the garden where Jesus would soon pray. The time was drawing near.

"Remember", He repeated, "you are not just writing for your time but for all times. When humanity faces its greatest challenge, they will need to rediscover My pure message-which you will record".

The disciples nodded solemnly. They were unaware that even as they sat there, Caiaphas- the high priest of Jerusalem- was already planning how to suppress the truths that Jesus had been teaching.

The Petrine Promise

CHAPTER 1: Saturday Evening

Evening light slanted through the stained-glass windows of The Church of Our Lady of the Assumption and the English Martyrs in Cambridge. It painted jewelled patterns across worn wooden pews. The scent of beeswax candles and ancient stone hung in the air, a fragrance Father Thomas had known for thirty years of ministry. But tonight, that familiar comfort felt hollow as he gazed out at the empty spaces in his congregation.

Twenty-three people. He'd counted them three times, though he wished he hadn't. Twenty-three, where once there had been hundreds. Their absence was as palpable as the silence between hymns. Each empty pew seemed to mock the hopes he'd once held for this parish.

At sixty-eight, Father Thomas carried his years in the smile lines around his eyes rather than in his bearing. Of medium height and slightly stooped from decades bent over manuscripts, he maintained the lean physique of someone who'd spent more time chasing ancient mysteries than indulging in earthly comforts. Wire-rimmed glasses and silver hair gave him a scholarly air but there was an intensity in his blue eyes that spoke of someone who'd found answers he'd never expected to find.

His hands, weathered by decades of turning scripture pages, holding communion chalices and indulging in his passion for archaeological digs, trembled slightly as he gripped the edges of the pulpit. Not from age- although now, he felt every year as it went by- but from the weight of what he'd discovered in his research.

"For our final reading this evening", he said, adjusting his glasses, "we turn to the Gospel of Matthew, Chapter Twenty-five, verses Thirty-one through Forty-six:

"'When the Son of man shall come in his glory, and all the holy angels with him, then shall he sit upon the throne of his glory:

And before him shall be gathered all nations: and he shall separate them one

from another, as a shepherd divideth his sheep from the goats:

And he shall set the sheep on his right hand, but the goats on the left.

Then shall the King say unto them on his right hand, Come, ye blessed of my Father, inherit the kingdom prepared for you from the foundation of the world:

For I was an hungred, and ye gave me meat: I was thirsty, and ye gave me drink: I was a stranger, and ye took me in:

Naked, and ye clothed me: I was sick, and ye visited me: I was in prison, and ye came unto me.

Then shall the righteous answer him, saying, Lord, when saw we thee an hungred, and fed thee? or thirsty, and gave thee drink?

When saw we thee a stranger, and took thee in? or naked, and clothed thee?

Or when saw we thee sick, or in prison, and came unto thee?

And the King shall answer and say unto them, Verily I say unto you, Inasmuch as ye have done it unto one of the least of these my brethren, ye have done it unto me.

Then shall he say also unto them on the left hand, Depart from me, ye cursed, into everlasting fire, prepared for the devil and his angels:

For I was an hungred, and ye gave me no meat: I was thirsty, and ye gave me no drink:

I was a stranger, and ye took me not in: naked, and ye clothed me not: sick, and in prison, and ye visited me not.

Then shall they also answer him, saying, Lord, when saw we thee an hungred, or athirst, or a stranger, or naked, or sick, or in prison, and did not minister unto thee?

Then shall he answer them, saying, Verily I say unto you, Inasmuch as ye did it not to one of the least of these, ye did it not to me.

And these shall go away into everlasting punishment: but the righteous into life eternal.'"

The words of judgment echoed through the vast space, Christ's message of accountability and social justice ringing as true now as it had two thousand years ago. *If only they understood what had been lost,* he thought. *What had been deliberately hidden.*

While he was reading, Father Thomas had occasionally stopped to glance at his small congregation. Most of them were elderly, fixtures of the parish for decades. But there in the back, a young mother with two children listened intently. Hunger for something real was visible in her eyes. They were all searching, he knew, even if they didn't fully understand what they were missing.

His voice echoed in the air. The evening light through the stained-glass windows continued to fall on the empty spaces, dust motes dancing in the coloured beams.

"Thank you for coming", he said softly to the congregation. "Go in peace. Love one another. Serve the LORD".

As the small congregation filed out, Michael Barnes, one of his lay readers, approached the pulpit. The younger man's face showed the same concern Father Thomas felt.

"Another drop from last week", Michael said quietly. "Remember when we had to add extra chairs for evening Mass?"

Father Thomas nodded, gathering his notes. "And it's not just us. Every church I know is facing the same decline. People want the hope that only a promise of justice can deliver- and they're not getting it in our teachings anymore".

"Yes, Father Thomas, I agree with you. Something is missing, isn't it? Something important".

"Though perhaps, not for much longer", Father Thomas replied, thinking of the research waiting in his office. It was more evidence that everything they had been taught had been deliberately altered.

Michael gave him a curious look but didn't press further. As the younger man walked away, Father Thomas remained at the pulpit, lost in thought. This latest evidence he'd discovered could change everything- but it could also destroy what little faith in Christianity remained. Was the world ready for what they'd found?

His phone buzzed in his pocket- another message from his contacts in Egypt. Something new had been discovered in the monastery archives, something that confirmed his worst fears. He needed to make some calls, especially to that brilliant young researcher at the British Museum, Dr. Chen. She had been his former student during her time at Cambridge University and they had stayed connected over the years. If his suspicions were correct, they would need her expertise in ancient languages.

His fingers lingered over Dr. Sarah Chen's number on his phone. Last week's conversation with his former student still echoed in his mind.

"I was thinking about our last conversation, Father Thomas", she'd said over coffee in the British Museum's café. "You remember we had been discussing Grigory Kessel's discovery of a hidden portion of a chapter of the Gospel of Matthew? I was wondering- could there be another reason for its existence other than the current scientific explanations? I noticed an interesting omission and I'm not sure if it is significant".

"Keep looking, Sarah", he'd told her, remembering his own discoveries. "Sometimes the most important truths hide in the smallest discrepancies".

Now, with what he'd found in his research, her expertise in ancient languages might be more crucial than either of them had ever realised. But first, he needed to confirm his suspicions about certain documents that shouldn't exist- documents that might explain why Christianity had changed so dramatically from its earliest years.

He'd contact her soon. For now, he needed to be certain of what he'd found. The consequences of being wrong- or worse of being right- were too grave to risk hasty action.

***

In the gathering darkness of Hyde Park, James Bradford's running shoes pounded against the path in rhythm with the bass line pulsing through his headphones. At forty, he carried himself with the easy confidence of someone who'd seen real danger and survived despite it. His dark hair was just beginning to grey at the temples, adding a distinguished touch to his rugged good looks, while his well-groomed beard enhanced rather than softened his sharp features His six-foot athletic frame moved with the fluid grace of his Royal Marines training.

Freddie Mercury's voice soared as he rounded the Serpentine, his mind shifting between the ancient texts he'd been studying and the growing evidence of something hidden in Christianity's earliest days.

"Another one bites the dust...". The lyrics seemed oddly appropriate, given what the

Guardians had discovered about early church history. James allowed himself a grim smile as he maintained his pace. Eight kilometres down, four to go. Running helped him think, helped him process the weight of the secrets he carried.

Other runners nodded as they passed, never guessing that the man in the faded Queen t-shirt and shorts was one of Britain's foremost religious historians. Or that he belonged to an organisation that had spent centuries protecting a truth that could change everything.

His dark eyes, holding both scholarly intelligence and something harder- the watchfulness of a man who knew too many secrets- scanned the path ahead. His phone buzzed with a message from his Guardian contacts. Unusual activity had been noted in the Vatican's archival division. James slowed to read it, then quickened his pace. Something was happening. Something they'd been waiting for.

***

Deep within the Vatican, Cardinal Romano sat at the head of an ancient oak table, its surface reflecting centuries of similar meetings. At sixty-three, he cut an imposing figure- tall and distinguished, with the bearing of someone who could have run a global business corporation instead of serving the Church. His meticulously maintained physique belied his age. His silver hair and aristocratic features gave him a statesman's presence- while his deep, resonant voice commanded attention without effort. The seven other Cardinals watched him in silence, their red robes appearing almost black in the chamber's dim light. A single hanging lamp cast a pool of illumination around him, leaving the room's corners in shadow.

Every Cardinal in the room had accepted a lifetime appointment for this particular task.

Cardinal Romano's grey eyes, capable of shifting from warmth to steel in an instant, surveyed the men before him. "Brothers", he said. His voice carried the weight of generations, "As we speak, another artefact is making its way to London, to the British

Museum, for evaluation". His fingers tensed as they traced the gold lettering on the worn brown leather notebook before him. The leather-bound notebook was in excellent condition, in spite of the fact that it was decades old. "We will have to do *everything* in our power to address the complications that will, most certainly, arise. It is our duty. Are you in agreement?"

The others nodded, their murmured responses echoing off stone walls that had heard countless secrets. "Whatever it takes".

"Yes". Cardinal Romano's eyes glinted in the lamplight. "Whatever it takes".

He closed the notebook with deliberate care, the sound echoing in the hushed chamber. "Now, duty calls", he said, rising from the table. The shadows seemed to move with him as he reached for his phone. "I must contact Luca immediately".

Alone in his office afterward, he paused before an ancient crucifix on the wall. His fingers touched the leather-bound Bible on his desk. It was different from his notebook, older. Much older. "Are we doing the right thing?" he whispered to himself in the empty room. He shook his head slightly, then straightened his shoulders and continued with his duties. There was no room for doubt. Not now.

***

In a cosy flat in Chelsea, Sarah Chen was curled up in her favourite reading chair. A glass of merlot was on the side table beside her. At thirty-five, she combined brilliant academic credentials with striking beauty-her Asian heritage giving her high cheekbones and elegant features that needed no enhancement. Long dark hair was pulled back in a practical style that suited both laboratory work and her natural grace. Her living room walls were lined with books-academic works on ancient languages, religious histories and archaeological texts. The room still smelled of the jasmine tea she had been drinking earlier. The scent of jasmine was mingled with the ever-present musty smell of old manuscripts that Sarah collected as a hobby.

Sarah picked up her glass to take another sip of wine and studied her notes. Since her last conversation with Father Thomas, she still hadn't solved the mystery.

She returned to the article in the journal she was reading. The journal was published by the Cambridge University Press and enjoyed a stellar academic reputation. Sarah checked the notes she had jotted down in her notebook:

#1- In 2023, Grigory Kessel was doing research in the Digital Vatican Library and discovered a portion of text- belonging to the Gospel of Matthew, Chapter 11:30 to 12:26. It was hidden as an underlayer of text in a 1,750-year-old Greek Bible manuscript.

#2- The Kessel text is written in the Old Syriac Aramaic language and has been determined to be at least one hundred years *older* than any other known Greek New Testament manuscripts, including the Codex Sinaiticus manuscript.

#3- The Kessel text is the lowest layer of writing (*scriptio ima*) on the page, with the text of the 1,750-year-old Greek Bible manuscript written over it.

#4- The Kessel text is not visible to the naked eye.

Sarah took another sip of wine and continued to read her notes:

#5- The Kessel translation is the fourth instance of independent manuscript evidence of Old Syriac Bibles that *pre-date* any Greek Bible manuscripts.

Sarah stopped reading and glanced at the framed photo on her bookshelf- herself at eight years old. She was sitting on her grandfather's lap in Hong Kong as he showed her characters in an ancient text. He'd sparked her love of languages, taught her that every symbol held meaning and every text told a story. What would he think of the puzzle she was trying to unravel now? Something about Kessel's discovery in the ancient manuscripts wouldn't let her rest.

Sarah headed to her bedroom, although she wasn't sleepy. *Okay- tomorrow, time for laundry*, Sarah reminded herself. On

Monday, she'd be back at her job in the religious documents lab at the British Museum.

***

None of them slept well that night.

Father Thomas sat in his study until dawn, surrounded by his research. James- having run until his legs ached, had only managed to get a few hours' sleep. Even Cardinal Romano, normally an excellent sleeper, tossed and turned all night. Sarah- eventually fell asleep and dreamt of ancient documents with their secrets waiting to be uncovered.

That night, little did any of them realise how big the storm was that was waiting for them, a storm they were each about to enter.

Sunday morning dawned grey and cool, typical English weather for March that matched the sombre mood in Father Thomas's office as he made one final call. In Hyde Park, James checked his encrypted messages while stretching out his running- weary muscles. More running was needed.

And in her flat, Sarah gathered her notes together for work on Monday, unaware that her quiet academic life was about to change forever.

None of them knew it yet, but their paths were about to converge around a truth that had been hidden for two thousand years. A truth that some might kill to keep secret, while others would be willing to die for in their fight to expose it.

The chase was about to begin.

The Petrine Promise

CHAPTER 2: The Fragment

Sarah arrived early at the British Museum, her footsteps echoing through marble corridors still hushed with pre-opening quiet. She loved this time of day, before the visitors filled the galleries- when she could almost hear the whispers of history in the air.

The grand edifice in Bloomsbury had stood as London's temple of knowledge since 1759, when Sir Hans Sloane's vast collection of curiosities first opened to the public. Now, nearly three centuries later, it remains one of the world's pre-eminent museums, drawing over six million visitors annually through its iconic colonnade entrance. The building itself, with its Greek Revival architecture and vast glass-ceilinged Great Court, housed a staggering eight million artefacts under the care of more than a thousand specialists, curators and support staff.

Sarah often reflected on how the museum's very existence spoke to humanity's need to preserve its past. While the Louvre might claim more visitors and the Metropolitan Museum of Art more American donors, the British Museum held something unique: the world's most comprehensive record of human civilisation, from the Rosetta Stone to the Parthenon sculptures. As she made her way past the sleeping galleries, their display cases holding treasures from every corner of the globe, she felt what she always felt-privilege mingled with responsibility. Here, in this hushed morning hour, she was part of an unbroken chain of scholars stretching back through centuries, all dedicated to preserving humanity's cultural heritage.

Her security card beeped her through a series of doors leading to the conservation labs, each threshold taking her further and further from the public spaces into the hidden world where the real work happened.

***

In his Vatican office, Cardinal Romano made two calls. The first was to Dr. Harrison.

"Nigel". The Cardinal's deep voice carried both warmth and warning. "I understand you have an interesting artefact being delivered today. I trust you have received my message about my requirements?"

"Yes, Your Eminence". Harrison's voice held the careful deference of someone who knew precisely where his funding came from. Although, he couldn't help wondering- *how had the Cardinal heard about this new fragment so quickly?* "The fragment will be in Dr. Chen's lab within the hour".

"Excellent. And you remember our arrangement?"

"Of course. I'll ensure you receive immediate word of anything she discovers". A pause "Though perhaps if I knew what we were looking for..."

"You'll know it when you see it, Nigel. Just as you've known other things over the years". The Cardinal's tone made it clear the conversation was ending. "I expect to hear from you soon".

His second call was to a number he rarely used but knew by heart. It was unlisted in any public phone directory.

"Luca". No warmth this time, only authority. "You need to be at the British Museum. Immediately".

"Yes, Your Eminence?" A voice as sharp as steel responded.

"An artefact. It will be in Dr. Chen's lab or on her person later today. It must be retrieved at all costs". As he spoke, the Cardinal's fingers traced the gold lettering on his notebook. "Though hopefully without any loss of life".

"Understood".

"Make sure you do. The artefact cannot, I repeat, cannot be allowed to get into the wrong hands. I, myself, will be travelling to the Museum this evening. I will expect your full report and to collect the artefact from you when I arrive".

"It will be done, Your Eminence".

The Cardinal ended the call, his grey eyes fixed on the ancient buildings visible through his window. Everything was in motion now. He could only pray they would have no unexpected loss of life.

***

As the morning sun filtered through the lab's high windows, Sarah settled at her workstation. The smell of preservation chemicals mixed with the musty scent of ancient parchment produced a fragrance more intoxicating to her than the finest French perfume. She was halfway through her morning tea when Dr. Harrison appeared.

"Dr. Chen". The head of Biblical Artefacts looked more dishevelled than usual, his bow tie slightly askew. "Glad I caught you early. We've had a priority acquisition come in- a new Dead Sea Scroll fragment that needs immediate examination and preservation. Apparently, it was discovered during the renovations of an ancient storage area beneath St. Catherine's Monastery".

Sarah's pulse quickened. In her ten years at the museum, she'd handled countless precious manuscripts but the Dead Sea Scrolls were her special favourite. "Authentication confirmed?"

"Preliminary tests look promising". He placed a sealed conservation case on her desk. "Carbon dating and material analysis support first-century origin. But there's something unusual about this one. The Vatican's Archaeological Commission has expressed particular interest. They've requested immediate updates on anything you find".

Sarah frowned. The Vatican rarely showed such interest in individual fragments. "Any idea why this one's so important?"

"None". Harrison wouldn't quite meet her eyes. "Just... handle this one carefully, Sarah. More carefully than usual".

He left her with the case and a growing sense that something wasn't quite right. Pushing the feeling aside, she began her standard protocols. The lab's fluorescent lights hummed overhead as she prepared her workspace, laying out tools with surgical precision. Her grandfather's voice echoed in her memory: *'Respect the text, little one. Every ancient word is a treasure waiting to be found'.*

The fragment itself was smaller than her palm. The parchment was dark with age but remarkably well-preserved. Sarah adjusted her microscope and began the painstaking process of documentation. She moved with the deliberate precision of someone used to handling priceless artefacts. Hours went by as her camera clicked rhythmically. She had to photograph every millimetre of the artefact, to build a digital record before attempting any preservation work.

That's when she saw it.

"This can't be right", she muttered, adjusting the microscope's focus. There, in the corner of the scroll's backing, barely visible to the naked eye, was something that shouldn't exist: a single tiny letter in ancient Aramaic. Its presence pointed to what appeared to be a hidden pocket in the scroll's binding.

Her hands trembled slightly as she reached for finer tools. Aramaic- the language Jesus actually spoke, not the Greek of later translations. She was one of only a handful of scholars worldwide qualified to read the oldest forms of this ancient language. The British Museum had hired her specifically for this expertise but in her ten years, she'd never seen anything quite like this.

Working with painstaking care, she loosened the delicate fibres of the binding. A small piece of papyrus slipped free, covered in precise Aramaic handwriting that looked remarkably well-preserved for its age. The script was elegant, clearly the work of a trained scribe.

Her heart raced as she started typing the translation of the first line:

'To those who seek truth: What you have been taught is not what was written..."

Sarah's hand froze above her keyboard. The implications of those words... She forced herself to continue typing, her fingers flying across the keys as the ancient text revealed its secrets:

'I, Ed-Tzdeik bar Yair, former scribe of the Temple, write this testimony knowing my life is forfeit. Caiaphas fears the spread of the Apostles' writings. Their message of social justice threatens those in power. But worse, in his view, is their insistence on personal accountability before God...'

The letter's next section made her inhale sharply:

'I witnessed the meeting where Caiaphas recruited Saul of Tarsus. "Become one of them. Create new writings", he commanded. "Shift their focus from the Father to the Son. Write to confuse. Write in a manner such that many will struggle to understand- especially the unlearned and the easily led. Add new doctrines to obscure the Apostles' simple message. And make salvation a matter of faith alone, not works, so they stop questioning our authority and our actions."'

She sat back, her mind reeling. *If this letter was authentic, it was exposing a deliberate conspiracy to alter Christianity from its very beginnings. Had they systematically changed Christ's message? Was Yair an actual eyewitness? Did he have any evidence of this conspiracy?*

As these questions swirled in her head, Sarah reached for her phone to text Dr. Harrison but stopped mid-motion. Something about this felt different. Important. Dangerous, even. She'd read enough Gary McAvoy novels and David Leadbeater novels and she'd seen enough Indiana Jones movies to know there was a grey area between reality and fiction. All ancient conspiracies had a basis in facts...

Her phone buzzed- a text from James Bradford. Even seeing his name made her pulse jump, though she'd never admit it. Three years of arguing over coffee in the museum café had taught her that the brilliant historian was both infuriating and infuriatingly attractive.

'Still working late?', his message read. 'Thought I saw your light on. Coffee?'

Sarah ignored the message and turned back to the translation. The ancient scribe's words pulled her deeper:

'But there were those who knew. Those who preserved the true testimonies. We hid copies in places they would never think to search, using the ancient symbols of our fathers. But most crucial are the records we kept of their plan. Each step, each change, each deliberate alteration of Christ's message From the first letters Saul wrote, to the final manipulation that would come at...'

The text ended abruptly at a tear in the papyrus. Sarah swore softly. Crucial information about the details of the final manipulation was lost.

Her phone buzzed again. Another text message. This time it was from Dr. Harrison 'Vatican delegation arriving in 20 minutes. Cardinal Romano leading them'.

Sarah's fingers flew faster across the keys, desperate to document everything before they arrived. Then, footsteps echoed in the museum's marble hallway- determined footsteps. Too soon.

She quickly slipped the papyrus into her tablet case just as Dr. James Bradford appeared in her doorway. Perfect timing, as always.

"Dr. Chen". He leaned against the doorframe, his dark eyes taking in the organised chaos of her workspace. "Still working on the new scroll fragment?"

Sarah fought the urge to smooth her hair. James Bradford was everything she usually avoided in a man- arrogant, sceptical and annoyingly handsome in that rugged way. He actually reminded her of another James- *Bond. James Bond,* she thought to herself and smiled. Although James Bradford did not exude a 'tuxedo and shaken martinis' aura- unlike his namesake. Sarah had noticed that there was still something quite dangerous about him.

Dr. Bradford specialised in disproving the authenticity of religious artefacts, which made him both the last person she wanted to talk to about her discovery and possibly the only one who could help verify it.

"Just finishing up", she said, trying to sound casual. "And please, after three years of arguing over coffee in the museum café, you can call me Sarah".

He smiled that infuriating half-smile that always made her stomach flutter. "Ok. Sarah, then". He stepped into the lab. "Speaking of coffee, I was wondering if---"

The lights went out.

In the sudden darkness, Sarah heard the faint sound of heavy footsteps coming down the hallway. They were too heavy for the museum's night guards.

James was already moving. "Back door", he whispered, reaching for her hand. "Now".

As they slipped out the lab's rear entrance, Sarah realised two things: she was still holding James's hand and her quiet academic life had just become extremely complicated.

The emergency lights cast an eerie red glow in the service corridor as they hurried toward the staff exit. Sarah's heart pounded, though whether from fear or his hand still gripping hers, she wasn't quite sure.

"Wait", James whispered, pulling her into a supply closet. The space was tight, forcing them close together. Sarah could smell his cologne- something expensive and distinctly masculine. He pressed a finger to his lips as heavy footsteps passed their hiding place.

"Friends of yours?" he murmured, his breath warm against her ear.

"I was about to ask you the same thing". Sarah tried to ignore how his body felt pressed against hers. "The Vatican's Archaeological Commission has been surprisingly interested in this scroll fragment".

"The Vatican?" His eyebrows rose. "Sarah, what exactly did you find?"

Before she could answer, her phone started vibrating. A text from Father Thomas, her old professor from Cambridge: 'URGENT. Need to speak with you. Don't trust anyone'.

The footsteps were returning.

"Do you trust me?" James asked suddenly, his dark eyes intense in the dim light.

"That's a loaded question for someone I've only argued with over coffee".

"Yet here we are, hiding in a closet". His lips twitched into that infuriating half-smile. "I know a place we can go. A safe house of sorts. But we need to move now".

The footsteps were getting closer. Sarah thought of the papyrus in her tablet case, with its mysterious message about truth and deception. She thought of Father Thomas's warning.

"Lead the way, Dr. Bradford".

His smile widened. "James", he corrected and then he was pulling her toward the emergency exit, into the rainy London night and straight into what would become either the greatest discovery in Christian history- or their death sentence.

The rain had soaked both of them by the time James led her to his Jaguar F-Type parked two blocks from the museum. The sleek black car purred to life as Sarah checked her tablet case- the papyrus was safe and dry.

"Nice car for a historian", she commented as they pulled into London traffic.

"Nice observation for someone who's not telling me what we're running from". He navigated smoothly through the wet streets, checking the rearview mirror frequently. "Though I'm guessing it has something to do with that papyrus you're clutching like it's the Holy Grail".

Sarah hesitated. In the warm interior of the car, with rain streaming down the windows, the events in the lab felt almost surreal. "How did you know it was a papyrus? Would you believe me if I said it might be more important than the Holy Grail?"

"To your first question- I have my sources". He turned onto a less travelled street. "To your second- coming from anyone else, no. But you're the most rigorous researcher I know. You don't jump at shadows or chase religious fairy tales".

"Is that why you've been arguing with my findings for three years?"

"I've been trying to get your attention for three years", he corrected, as he turned to look deeply into her eyes. "The arguments were just a bonus".

Before Sarah could process that revelation, headlights blazed behind them- a black SUV was gaining speed.

James swore softly. "Hold on".

The Jaguar surged forward, engine growling as they wove through traffic. Sarah gripped her seat as James demonstrated driving skills that were definitely not learned in academia.

"MI6?" she asked, only half-jokingly.

"Former Royal Marines. Before I decided ancient history was more interesting than modern conflicts". He took a sharp turn down an alley. "Your turn. What's in the papyrus?"

The SUV was still behind them. As Sarah held her tablet case, her hands shook slightly. "It's a letter, first century, hidden in the scroll fragment's binding. According to this, Caiaphas and Paul deliberately added books to the New Testament- books that weren't written by Christ's actual Apostles. By doing this, they systematically changed the original message.

"The letter also claims Caiaphas and Paul deliberately..." She stopped as another SUV appeared ahead of them, blocking the street.

James's face was grim as he checked his mirrors. "We're about to have company, Sarah. Whatever's in that letter, someone obviously doesn't want it found". He reached across her to open the glove compartment, revealing a handgun. "Last chance to tell me you're secretly an international spy".

"Sorry to disappoint. Just a boring academic who may have stumbled onto the biggest cover-up in Christian history". She tried to smile but her heart was racing.

"Nothing boring about you, Dr. Chen". James's eyes met hers again for a moment, intense and searching, before returning to the approaching vehicles. "Now, about that safe house I mentioned..."

The SUVs were closing in from both directions. Sarah clutched her tablet case and nodded. "Drive".

The Jaguar fishtailed around a corner, spraying water across the pavement. Sarah's phone buzzed again- another text from Father Thomas: 'GET OUT NOW.'

"Problem?" James asked, smoothly manoeuvring between two buses.

"It's Father Thomas", showing him the text. "He never sends messages like this".

"Then your discovery is even more significant than you realise". James pressed the accelerator harder. "Trust me, we need to keep moving".

"Ok. I trust you but they're right behind us!" Sarah gasped as they flew around another corner.

"That's strange", James said moments later. "They've had at least three clear shots at us since the museum. Vatican security forces don't typically hesitate".

"What are you saying?"

"I'm saying they might not be trying to eliminate us. Maybe just contain us. Or…" his brow furrowed, "direct us".

"To what end?" Sarah asked.

James shook his head. "I don't know and that is what's worrying me".

The SUVs were falling behind but Sarah had a feeling this was just the beginning. She studied James's profile as he drove, noting how his scholarly demeanour had shifted to something more dangerous, more compelling. What other secrets was Dr. Bradford hiding?

A flash of movement caught her eye. "Motorcycle, coming up fast".

James checked his mirrors and swore softly. "Time for plan B". He continued driving for another minute and then made a sharp turn into what appeared to be a solid brick wall- but the holographic projection dissolved around them, revealing a hidden entrance to an underground parking facility.

"MI6 might have been an understatement", Sarah managed as the wall re-materialised behind them.

James parked and turned to her, his expression serious. "There are organisations within organisations, Sarah. Some want the truth found. Others...". He glanced at her tablet case.

"According to the letter, after adding additional books to the New Testament, Caiaphas went on to set in motion a final manipulation. James- what do you think it was?"

"That's what we have to find out, Sarah", James answered, as they both climbed out of the car.

The hunt for truth had begun. And somewhere in the rainy London night, ancient secrets were waiting to be found.

The Petrine Promise

CHAPTER 3: The Safe House

The safe house turned out to be a converted warehouse in Bermondsey, in southeast London. Its industrial exterior concealed a sophisticated interior that looked more like a high-tech research facility than a hideout. The contrast between the building's weathered Victorian brick and the cutting-edge security systems reminded Sarah of James himself- scholarly refinement masking something far more dangerous.

"Welcome to my other office", James said, leading her through a retinal scanner. Blue light washed over them as hidden cameras tracked their movement. "The official version is that I consult for various museums on security matters".

"And the unofficial version?" Sarah watched him punch in a complex code, noting how naturally he moved through these layers of security. The James Bradford she thought she knew- the argumentative historian who debated theology over coffee- was revealing new depths with every passing minute.

He smiled that infuriating half-smile again. "Let's focus on your discovery first". They emerged into a vast open space filled with state-of-the-art equipment.

"Ah, Malcolm!" James called out to a figure hunched over a complex array of monitors. "I hoped you'd be here. We need your help with something delicate".

The man straightened, revealing an attractive face with bright, intelligent eyes behind round horn-rimmed glasses. Despite his rumpled cardigan and unbuttoned shirt, there was something sharp and precise about his movements as he approached.

"Dr. Chen, meet Malcolm Blackwood. Former MI6 tech division, now our resident genius at making ancient and modern play nicely together. Malcolm, meet Dr. Sarah Chen from the British Museum".

"Charmed", Malcolm said, his crisp Oxford accent at odds with his dishevelled appearance. His eyes had already fixed on Sarah's tablet case with an almost predatory interest. "That wouldn't happen to be a first-century document in need of non-invasive spectral imaging, would it?"

James drew Malcolm aside, their voices dropping to whispers. Sarah caught fragments: "...diplomatic credentials..." "...secure transport to Egypt..." "...off the standard channels..."

Malcolm nodded, already tapping commands into a wrist-mounted device that looked nothing like any smartwatch Sarah had ever seen. "Give me an hour. Oh, and James?" He glanced at Sarah, then back to James with a half-smile that didn't quite reach his eyes. "Do try not to get shot this time. The paperwork's dreadful".

Banks of monitors lined one wall, while preservation chambers that would make the British Museum envious occupied another. At the centre stood a document examination station that looked military grade. James turned to Sarah, "Show me what's got the Vatican so worried they're sending agents at night to the British Museum. What did you find?"

Sarah carefully removed the papyrus and placed it under a digital scanner. Ancient Aramaic text filled the high-resolution screen, the characters crisp and clear under the advanced imaging system.

"It's written in Aramaic- the actual language Jesus and His disciples spoke", she explained, her fingers tracing the characters on the screen. "That's significant in itself. Almost everything we have from this period was preserved in Greek text".

"Why is that significant?" James moved closer, his shoulder brushing hers as he studied the text. The contact sent a jolt through her that had nothing to do with ancient manuscripts.

"Because it's probably an actual eyewitness account of the conspiracy". Sarah's voice tightened with tension as she began translating. "It's from someone named Yair, a scribe in Jerusalem's temple. His name is Aramaic not Hebrew. But he must have known how to write Hebrew really well to have been working in the Temple. He documented exactly how Caiaphas and Saul of Tarsus- who later became Paul- planned to change Christianity".

She adjusted the imaging settings, which revealed layers of text that had been undetected by the Museum's scanner. "According to this, Caiaphas was already alarmed by how quickly Jesus's message had resonated with the crowds. His alarm was growing even more urgent as he realised how quickly the Apostles' Aramaic writings were spreading. Remember, they too, were repeating Jesus's emphasis on social justice and personal accountability. So, Caiaphas decided to intervene. Yair kept notes of Caiaphas' meetings, his plans to add new writings and his deliberate effort to shift focus away from Christ's original message".

"Hence their Greek translations?" James's scholarly instincts were clearly engaged now. His expertise in early church history was evident in the questions he asked.

"Exactly". Sarah pulled up comparative texts on adjacent screens. "The letter claims Caiaphas recruited Saul. Then, they deliberately chose to promote Paul's new

Greek writings while suppressing the Apostles' original Aramaic testimonies. It wasn't just about modifying the original message- it was about erasing the evidence that a different message had ever existed".

Her fingers flew across the keyboard as she continued translating. "Yair says they specifically introduced new concepts that weren't in any of the apostolic writings---"

"Like what exactly?"

"Like the Trinity doctrine. They planted the idea that Jesus is God. This was supposed to shift focus away from the Father and create enough doctrinal confusion to divide believers".

"Making the truth harder to find", James murmured. "Hidden under layers of translation and tradition". He reached past her to adjust one of the monitors, his proximity making it hard for her to concentrate. "Look at this section- the scribe is describing specific meetings".

Sarah nodded, forcing herself to focus on the text rather than James's closeness. "He names witnesses, locations, dates. This isn't just an accusation- it's detailed testimony from someone who was there, someone who---"

James's phone buzzed, cutting her off. The message turned his expression grim. "Sarah, Father Thomas is missing. And, according to my contact, someone accessed the restricted archives beneath the Vatican's Aramaic manuscripts collection".

"They're looking for more letters", Sarah realised. the implications hitting her. "This letter... it's not just a warning. It's a sign, isn't it? Of other documents?"

"The question is", James said, checking his weapon. "can we find them first?"

Sarah turned back to the scanner, scrolling through the text. "There's something else here... references to locations. Alexandria, yes, but also..." her voice dropped to a whisper. "The Tomb of Joseph of Arimathaea".

"The man who buried Christ". James leaned in closer, his presence both distracting and reassuring. "What does it say about him?"

"According to this, Joseph wasn't just a wealthy supporter. He was part of a secret group within the Sanhedrin who recognised Jesus as the prophesied Messiah. After the crucifixion, he didn't just provide his tomb-he also provided a secure location for preserving the Apostles' original manuscripts and other documents. He protected the evidence that a different New Testament message had existed first".

Sarah's mind raced with possibilities. "James, if this is true... if Joseph of Arimathaea really hid evidence of how they changed Christianity---"

A loud bang echoed through the warehouse above them. James immediately moved to a security panel, checking cameras. Modern and ancient collided again as he switched between thermal imaging and standard views.

"We've got company. Three teams. Professional setup. We've got two minutes tops". He grabbed a laptop and began downloading the scanned document. "How good is your Aramaic on the move?"

Sarah put the papyrus back in her tablet case and clutched it to her chest. "Good enough. But we may need help. Father Thomas has connections with the Aramaic church in northern Iraq. If he's missing..."

"Then that's where they'll expect us to go". James finished the download and handed her a small backpack with the laptop inside. "Which is why we're going somewhere else first. How do you feel about Cambridge?"

"The University?"

"Yes and no". His smile had an edge to it now. "Actually, it's a secret library beneath the Chapel. Remember when I said there are organisations within organisations? It's time for you to see what the real historians have been up to".

As alarms began blaring through the facility, Sarah realised two things: she was about to be pulled into a world she never knew existed and Dr. James Bradford was far more than just a former Royal Marine turned scholar.

"Trust me?" he asked again, holding out his hand.

This time, she didn't hesitate. Whatever secrets James had been keeping, whatever world he was about to show her, one thing was clear- the truth about Christianity's transformation was finally coming to light. And someone was willing to kill to keep it hidden.

Sarah reflected on how her path had led her here. Her expertise in biblical artefacts hadn't been a random career choice. For years, she'd struggled with the contradictions she'd found in Christian teachings- the gap between Christ's simple message of love and justice and the complex doctrines that seemed to serve more earthly purposes. How Jesus had welcomed everyone, challenged social hierarchies and warned of a final judgment based on works, not mere belief. Yet, somehow, Sarah felt these fundamental truths had become buried beneath layers of later interpretation.

When friends or colleagues asked her about her faith, she'd learned to give careful answers. "I believe deeply in God and Christ and the Holy Spirit", she would say, "but I stopped attending church because I couldn't reconcile what I was hearing from the pulpit with what I was reading in the earliest texts". It was this disconnect that had drawn her to ancient manuscripts, seeking answers from the words of those who had walked with Jesus himself. Perhaps that's why Father Thomas had taken such an interest in her work- he'd recognised another seeker of truth.

Now, standing in this secret facility with James, Sarah felt a surge of certainty. The letter she'd discovered wasn't just of academic interest- it was an answer to questions she'd been asking herself her whole life. Whatever dangers lay ahead, she couldn't stop now- she had to discover the truth.

The warehouse's emergency lighting cast red shadows as James led them to what looked like a maintenance closet. Inside, he pressed his palm against a blank wall. A hidden elevator hummed to life.

"The thing about secret societies", he said, as they descended, "is that there's usually another secret society watching them. For every group that wanted to suppress the original teachings, another was working to preserve them".

"And which group are you with?" Sarah asked, noting how naturally he held his weapon and how calmly he moved in a crisis. This wasn't just training- this was years of experience.

"The Guardians of Truth. Interestingly, we trace our origins to Joseph of Arimathaea himself". The elevator continued its descent, taking them deeper beneath London's streets. "What you've discovered is part of something bigger, Sarah. A truth we've been protecting for centuries". He paused, choosing his next words carefully. "Have you ever heard of the LOGOS Bible?"

Sarah shook her head, watching James's face in the dim emergency lighting. The scholarly mask was gone now, replaced by something older, more purposeful.

"It's the original compilation, just---". A burst of gunfire above cut him off. "Story time later. Right now, we need to get to the tunnel system".

The elevator opened into a Victorian-era tunnel, its brick walls lined with modern fibre optic cables. The past and present merged again, just as they had in the safe house above.

"This is part of the Thames Tunnel, which was built in the 1800s". James explained as they hurried along. "It was converted to accommodate train lines and now..." He gestured to a sophisticated security door ahead. "It's one of only two access routes to one of the largest collections of pre-Nicene biblical manuscripts in the world".

Sarah's heart skipped a beat. "How is this not known?"

"The same way your letter stayed hidden-powerful people prefer that certain truths remain buried". James tapped in a code on the security panel next to the security door. The door opened to reveal a Jaguar I-PACE electric SUV parked in a modern concrete chamber. "Some of us disagree".

As they climbed into the silent vehicle, Sarah's phone lit up with a message. Her hands shook as she read it.

"James", she held up the phone, "it's from Father Thomas".

The message was in Aramaic:

"They're coming. Remember John 15:27".

Sarah stared at the ancient language glowing on her modern phone screen. Like everything else in this night of revelations, old and new were colliding in ways she never could have imagined. The truth about Christianity's transformation was finally emerging from the shadows.

And somehow, she knew, this was just the beginning.

The I-PACE moved silently through the tunnels, its headlights cutting through the darkness. Sarah studied the Aramaic message again.

"John 15:27", she murmured. "'And ye also shall bear witness, because ye have been with me from the beginning.' It's one of the verses where Jesus specifically commissioned the Apostles to record His teachings".

"And now, Father Thomas must have found incontrovertible proof that only the apostolic writings were meant to be included in the New Testament". James navigated a complex intersection of tunnels. "The later additions- Paul's letters, Mark, Luke and even the letter to the Hebrews- they were never meant to be part of the New Testament Canon".

"A deliberate effort to add non-apostolic writings..." Sarah's mind raced with implications. "James- his evidence will expose how traditional Christianity was deliberately led away from Christ's original message".

"You know, an attempt to expose the truth about the conspiracy almost happened once before". He pressed a button on the dash, bringing up a holographic map of the tunnel system. "In Cambridge, 1867. A group of scholars found similarly explosive evidence and were about to release it. But within three days, their library and its documentary evidence mysteriously burned down and the only survivor disappeared".

"Let me guess- the Guardians took him in?"

"Her, actually. Dr. Martha Morton. She became one of our most committed members". The tunnel ahead split into three paths. James took the rightmost one. "The world wasn't ready then. But now, with digital preservation, global communication..."

"And the Vatican moving to stop us", Sarah said, as she checked her phone again. "Hmm- no more messages from Father Thomas. The question is- why are they still trying to suppress this? After all this time?"

"Because it's not just about the past. Think about it- if people realised that core doctrines like the Trinity came from non-apostolic sources, if they understood how concepts like 'once saved, always saved' were added later..." James's eyes remained focused on the tunnel ahead. "It would force a complete re-evaluation of modern Christian practice".

"Back to Christ's original message of social justice and personal accountability", Sarah added. "The message Caiaphas feared would upset the power structure".

"Exactly. Some power structures haven't changed much in two thousand years".

Multiple vehicles suddenly blocked their path, their headlights blinding. A familiar voice crackled over their radio.

"Dr. Chen, Dr. Bradford. This is Cardinal Romano. I believe you have something that the Church needs to secure for safekeeping".

James switched off the I-PACE's lights, leaving them in shadow. "Any chance he means my overdue library books?"

"Dr. Chen", the Cardinal's voice came again. "The letter you found was never meant to be made public. Think of the chaos it would cause. The crisis of faith for millions of believers".

"Or the awakening", Sarah muttered. She turned to James and said, "Please tell me you have a plan B".

"The Guardians have been preparing for this moment for centuries". His hands moved across the dashboard, pressing a sequence of buttons. The tunnel floor beneath them suddenly shifted. Sarah grabbed the armrest as the I-PACE began to descend on a hidden hydraulic platform.

"The Romans. The Victorians. And all the way up to the cold war and beyond", James explained as they dropped below the main tunnel level, "they've all had to become particularly good at building things within things and connecting old things to new things".

Cardinal Romano's voice crackled with static. "You can't hide from us forever, Dr. Bradford".

"I don't intend to", James mumbled. To Sarah, he added, "What you're about to see isn't part of the 'London Bridge Experience & London Tombs tour'. Are you ready to see where the Guardians really keep their secrets?"

The platform locked into place, revealing yet another tunnel system that appeared to be much older than Victorian engineering.

"Medieval", Sarah breathed, recognising the stonework. "Original construction".

"Built by people who knew exactly which texts were supposed to be preserved". James guided the I-PACE forward. "And more importantly- why".

The Petrine Promise

CHAPTER 4: The Heart

The I-PACE's headlights illuminated ancient stone walls lined with symbols Sarah recognised from early Christian catacombs. But these were different- more detailed, more specific.

"These aren't just decorative", she said, leaning forward to study them as they drove. "They're markings... some kind of guide system?"

"The Guardians' original navigation code. Each symbol represents a different type of document or artefact". James slowed the vehicle. "See that one? The dove with a scroll? That marks repositories of apostolic writings".

A distant explosion echoed from above, sending dust filtering down from the medieval ceiling.

"They're not going to just let us go, are they?"

"The Vatican has spent centuries making sure certain truths stay hidden. They're not going to stop now". James checked a small device on the dashboard. "We have maybe twenty minutes before they find a way down here".

"Then we better hope whatever Father Thomas found is worth all this". Sarah studied the symbols again. "There- that chamber ahead has the dove mark".

The I-PACE stopped before a heavy wooden door reinforced with modern security technology. James pressed his palm to a hidden scanner.

"Sarah", he said as the door began to open, "what you're about to see... it's what the Guardians have been protecting. Evidence of how they systematically changed Christianity".

The ancient door swung open to reveal a vast circular chamber, its walls lined with preserved documents dating from the first to the fourth centuries. In the centre stood a massive stone table, its surface carved with the same symbolic language that marked the tunnels.

"Welcome to the Heart", James said softly. "This is where we've secured our gathered evidence- proof of how Christianity was deliberately altered".

Sarah moved towards the table, her trained eye taking in details that made her pulse quicken. "These are copies of letters, official correspondence... James, is that a personal letter from Caiaphas?"

"It's one of the ones his allies didn't manage to destroy". James activated a control panel, bringing the chamber's modern preservation systems to life. "For two thousand years, the Guardians have protected this evidence- in one way or another".

"Why wasn't any of it ever published", Sarah asked. "If even as a matter of public interest?"

"Sarah- we couldn't", James replied. "We had to wait for the right moment to expose the truth so as not to do more damage than good. Remember, many of our documents are copies. Some are authenticated. Some are not. But even if we had sworn statements, Affidavits, from eyewitnesses to authenticate every single incriminating document, that still wouldn't have been enough. These documents are too explosive.

"So, the Guardians decided to protect the evidence that we had gathered until original documents, corroborating what we had, came to light". James paused. "It was the best that we could do, under the circumstances. We felt, the bigger tragedy- would have been to release our information prematurely, only to have it be dismissed and discounted. So, each generation of Guardians before me has been watching and waiting".

Sarah exclaimed. "Ah- I understand now. That's why the Yair Letter is so important".

"Exactly". James replied. "It's an original document. Nobody can argue with that fact. So, the Yair Letter authenticates our documents, even though our documents are copies. Remember, in John's Gospel, Chapter Eleven, it revealed how Caiaphas, high priest of the Pharisees, felt after Christ raised Lazarus from the dead. That one miracle spurred him on to organise Christ's crucifixion. But even Caiaphas could not have predicted just how popular the apostolic writings would make Christ's message. In his mind, he had to respond. And respond he did, as the Yair Letter confirms`'.

Another explosion rumbled above, closer this time.

"We need to move quickly now". James crossed to a specific case. "Father Thomas's message isn't just about warning us. 'Remember John 15:27'. It's about proving who had the authority to write scripture".

The case opened with a soft hiss of preserved air. Inside lay a collection of documents that made Sarah hold her breath.

"Oh my gosh", she whispered, carefully examining one of the scrolls. "Look at this-this is another copy of correspondence between Caiaphas and Paul. It details how they planned to dilute the Apostles' message. And here- documents showing how they began circulating additional texts to communities of Christians..." Sarah paused, continuing to examine more documents.

"These are copies of the actual records of their plan- correspondence, meeting minutes, orders for new writings to be created. They documented everything".

A red light began pulsing on James's security device. "They're coming. Less than five minutes".

Sarah's fingers flew across the ancient text. "James, this proves everything. How they planned everything to deliberately alter Christ's original message".

"And that's exactly why they can't take the risk of letting the Yair Letter evidence get out". James pressed a sequence of symbols on the stone table. A section of the floor began to move, revealing a deep shaft with modern climbing gear. "A generation of Guardians added this- in the 1950s. It leads to a boat we keep on the River Thames".

Sarah carefully secured some of the documents in a waterproof case. "These letters reveal the plan, but there must be more. Was anybody else involved?"

"Yes". James handed her a climbing harness. The chamber door shuddered under a heavy impact.

"Let me guess", Sarah said, fastening the harness. "That's what Father Thomas went to confirm".

"And why they're so desperate to stop us. These documents prove the conspiracy began with Caiaphas and Paul. But it didn't end there". The door shuddered again.

"Sarah". James's eyes held hers. "If we expose this, it changes everything. People will finally understand why early Christianity spread so rapidly- because the Apostles' original message was about real transformation of the individual and the society".

"Not the modified message that came later", she finished.

He nodded. "Ready to make some history?"

The door burst open as they began their descent, Cardinal Romano's voice echoing through the chamber: "You have no idea what you're unleashing!"

71

But Sarah knew exactly what they were unleashing. Evidence that would prove the conspiracy and expose the additional books that had been added.

The truth couldn't be hidden any longer.

CHAPTER 5: Hidden in Plain Sight

The British Museum's conservation lab felt different in the pre-dawn hours. Sarah sat at her workstation. The Aramaic letter was now properly secured between preservation sheets. Her hands were steady but her mind raced with questions about the previous night's escape.

James had dropped her back at the museum with instructions to act normally- 'The best place to hide is in plain sight'. He was right, of course. No one would expect her to return to work after their dramatic flight through the tunnels.

The Letter lay before her, its ancient Aramaic text somehow more ominous in the early morning light. She began a systematic translation, her fingers moving across her keyboard:

> 'To those who seek truth: What you have been taught is not what was written. I, Ed-Tzdeik bar Yair, former scribe of the Temple, write this testimony knowing my life is forfeit.

Caiaphas fears the spread of the Apostles' writings. Their message of social justice threatens those in power. But worse, in his view, is their insistence on personal accountability before God...'

Sarah paused, double-checking her translation.

'I witnessed the meeting where Caiaphas recruited Saul of Tarsus. "Create new writings", he commanded. "Shift their focus from the Father to the Son. Write to confuse. Write in a manner such that many will struggle to understand you- especially the unlearned and the easily led. Add new doctrines to obscure the Apostles' simple message. And make salvation a matter of faith alone, not works, so they stop questioning our authority..."'

Her phone buzzed- a text from James: 'Vatican delegation arriving at Museum in 30 minutes. Cardinal Romano leading them.

Get what you can and meet me at the arranged location.'

Sarah's fingers flew faster across the keys.

Footsteps echoed in the corridor outside.

Sarah quickly photographed the Letter with her phone, then began the standard conservation process as Dr Harrison, the head of Biblical Artefacts, entered with three men in dark suits. Cardinal Romano's silver hair gleamed under the lab lights.

"Dr. Chen". The Cardinal's smile didn't reach his eyes. "I understand you have made an interesting discovery".

"Just routine conservation work", Sarah replied, keeping her voice steady. "A Dead Sea Scroll fragment requiring standard preservation and a papyrus with Aramaic writing".

"May we?" The Cardinal gestured towards the Museum's ultraviolet light digital imaging scanner.

"Of course", Sarah stepped aside, grateful she'd already documented the text. "Though

I should warn you, the material is quite fragile".

He bent over to look into the scanner, his expression changing as he read the Aramaic. When he straightened, his friendly demeanour had vanished.

"Where is the rest of it?"

"I'm sorry?"

"Dr. Chen, surely you understand the significance of what you've found. The trouble it could cause if misinterpreted". He gestured to his companions. "The Vatican would like to take custody of this artefact. For proper study, of course".

"That would be highly irregular", Sarah began but Dr. Harrison interrupted.

"I'm afraid I've already approved the transfer", he said, not meeting her eyes. "Sarah- you know that Cardinal Romano is the head of the Vatican Apostolic Archive. The Vatican's resources for studying materials of this period are unmatched".

Sarah watched helplessly as one of the Cardinal's men carefully lifted the preservation case containing the Letter. The Cardinal turned to her again.

"We would also appreciate your expertise in this matter. Perhaps you'd consider accompanying us to Rome? Your knowledge of ancient Aramaic would be invaluable".

The threat was clear beneath the invitation. They wanted her where they could watch her.

"That's very kind", Sarah said, "but I have commitments here that can't be broken".

"Pity". His smile returned, cold as marble. "Should you change your mind, the offer remains open. Though I should mention- we're also quite interested in speaking to Dr Bradford about his... extracurricular activities".

They left her standing in the lab, her phone burning in her pocket with the photographed evidence. As soon as their footsteps faded, she sent a quick text to James: 'They have the letter. But we still have the translation. Meet now?'

His reply came instantly: 'King's College Chapel. 3 hours. Watch your back.'

Sarah gathered her things, mind racing. The Yair Letter had mentioned records- detailed evidence of a final manipulation. If they could find those records...

But first, she had to get out of the Museum without being followed. And based on the way the Cardinal's men had positioned themselves in the corridor, that wasn't going to be easy.

CHAPTER 6: The Vatican Secret Archive

With the Yair Letter in his possession, Cardinal Romano decided it was time to fly back to Rome. He knew he had to secure the artefact and then update His Holiness, the Pope, on recent developments.

He settled back into his airplane seat and admitted to himself that it would be good to get back home to the peacefulness of his office at the Vatican. As the years went by, he was finding it harder and harder to deal with the stress of his duties.

As he closed his eyes to take a nap, his mind journeyed back to the history of the Vatican and its secret documents.

The very first Bishop of Rome, St. Peter, one of Christ's named Apostles, had amassed a large collection of secret documents. Of course, his first responsibility was to ensure the safe storage of the apostolic testimonies. And he had seen to that. However, as time passed, numerous additional documents entered the Pope's

79

possession. They, too, required safeguarding.

Before the formal Library in the Vatican even existed- the first Popes had kept all their documents together as a collection. This collection was known as the Holy Scrinium or the Chartarium.

For fourteen centuries, little had changed in this system. On St. Peter's death, and the death of all subsequent Popes, the document collection simply passed from one Pope to his successor for safekeeping.

However, in 1475, the construction of the Vatican Library was finally completed and the storage of the Pope's documents became much more formalised. The Vatican Library was always supervised by a Cardinal who was given the title of Vatican Librarian.

However, as each successive Vatican Librarian took office, it became apparent that highly sensitive classified documents should not be mixed up with other, more mundane documents.

Thus, in 1612, less than two hundred years after the official opening of the Vatican Library, Pope Paul V ordered the creation of the 'Vatican Secret Archive'. All documents, in any way related to the Apostles, were transferred from the Vatican Library to be housed exclusively in this new private and secret library.

Since Pope Paul V's papacy, the Vatican Secret Archive has operated independently of the main Vatican Library. Furthermore, as the ownership of the documents and artefacts in this Secret Archive are vested in the Pope, only His Holiness has the authority to release these secret documents or any information about these secret documents into the public domain.

Cardinal Romano stirred. He woke up and requested an expresso from the flight staff. He was feeling very tired. As he sipped the hot coffee, he continued to reflect on recent events at the Vatican.

He thought of himself as a traditionalist. Nevertheless, he understood what Pope Francis had hoped to achieve when he ordered a name change from the 'Vatican

Secret Archive' to the 'Vatican Apostolic
Archive' in 2019.

And, in a spirit of transparency, the Pope
had even authorised limited access to some
of the documents being kept in the newly
named Vatican Apostolic Archive. Cardinal
Romano knew that it was because of this in
procedure that Grigory Kessel had been
granted access to the 1,750-year-old Greek
Bible manuscript in 2023. Access to this
document allowed Kessel to discover the
Syriac undertext of part of the Gospel of
Matthew underneath the Greek biblical text.

The memory of that discovery woke
Cardinal Romano from his sleepy
recollections. That discovery had re-ignited
heated worldwide discussions regarding the
authenticity of the first-century Greek New
Testament manuscripts.

The Cardinal shifted his body weight and
turned towards the window at his right. He
looked outside. It was a nice day and they
were flying above the clouds. His watch told
him- he would be landing in Rome in less
than 2 hours.

Once again, he leaned back into his seat and
reflected on his long career in the Church.

He had decided to become a priest at an
early age and against his father's wishes.
But it was all he had ever wanted to do- he
loved the certainty that his faith gave him.
His father was a Prosecutor, so at least they
shared a love of ritual and justice. Cardinal
Romano had always understood, even as a
young man, that a theme of justice united
the first book of the Bible to the last.

By nature, he had always been meticulous,
ambitious and much better with paperwork
than with people. A fact that had been
recognised by church observers thirty-five
years ago- when he was first transferred
from his pastoral duties to work in the main
Vatican Library.

The Cardinal frowned and opened his eyes
briefly to look around the plane. He shifted
his body again and then closed his eyes as
he continued with his recollections. He
never called the Vatican Library- 'the Vat',
as some were accustomed to doing. His
respect for the institution demanded his use
of its proper name- the Vatican Library- at
all times.

His instinctive discretion, appreciation for matters of State and his imposing presence had made his subsequent transfer to the Vatican Secret Archive a foregone conclusion. Now, years later, as the head of this Secret Archive, he reported directly to the Pope- just as all his predecessors before him had done.

Every head of the Secret Archive inherits seven Cardinals who assist him in his work. These Cardinals enjoy lifetime appointments. When one of these Cardinals dies, His Holiness- at his sole discretion, appoints a replacement.

This practice of a lifetime assignment is in direct contrast to what typically happens to Cardinals working in other departments in the Vatican. Although elevation to a Cardinal is a lifetime recognition, Cardinals usually serve a five-year term in their departmental assignments. Sometimes, these assignments can be renewed for an additional five-year term.

However, the Cardinals assigned to the Vatican Secret Archive and the Cardinal who heads the Apostolic Penitentiary are exempt from these term restrictions. Confidentiality and continuity of service were deemed of the utmost importance here.

Each of the eight Cardinals working in the Secret Archive is responsible for a different area. Cardinal Rossi, for example, monitored new book publications. A synopsis of every book published each week, anywhere in the world, in any language, is prepared by his Vatican team for analysis and digital filing in the Secret Archive. Cardinal Kaguma, from Uganda, monitored the research results on apocryphal documents. Similarly, the other five Cardinals all had areas of special responsibility.

In addition to being the head of the Secret Archive, Cardinal Romano's specific area of responsibility was monitoring the classified documents section of the Secret Archive. Because this was his area of responsibility, he was looking forward to completing the delivery of the Yair Letter artefact.

As he sat up and stretched his legs, he noted that the plane would be landing in 15 minutes. His audience with the Pope had already been scheduled.

At the end of his audience with His Holiness, he anticipated being asked the same question the Pope always asked him, under these extraordinary circumstances, "Are you sure that we are doing the right thing?"

It was a question he did not like to be asked. There was no right answer.

He sent Luca a quick text message with new instructions and then quickly reviewed his notes on the events of the last few days. He had written his notes, as he always did, in his worn brown leather-bound notebook. When he finished checking his notes, he closed the notebook and traced the gold lettering on its cover with his fingers.

As he relaxed backwards into his seat again, Cardinal Romano hoped that the discovery of the Yair Letter by Dr. Chen, and his subsequent acquisition of it, had ended yet another narrow escape for the Church.

He was wrong.

CHAPTER 7: The Chase

The British Museum's Central Court echoed with the first visitors of the day as Sarah Chen walked purposefully toward the main entrance, her tablet case clutched close. Her heart raced beneath her carefully maintained calm exterior. Through the glass ceiling high above, storm clouds gathered over London.

She'd nearly reached the Great Russell Street exit when she saw them- two men in dark suits who moved nothing like tourists. Their earpieces and vigilant eyes marked them as part of the Vatican's surveillance team. A third man appeared at the north entrance, then a fourth by the gift shop.

Sarah forced herself not to react. Instead, she pulled out her phone as if checking for messages, using its screen to observe the men's reflections. They were coordinating their movements, steadily closing in. But Sarah had an advantage they didn't know about- the benefit of working for ten years in this labyrinth of a building.

She turned abruptly, heading for the Egyptian galleries. The agents followed, trying to look casual among the morning crowds. Sarah slipped between two massive sarcophagi, then ducked through a staff door hidden behind a display case. The security guard nodded- he knew her well.

The service corridors were a maze unto themselves, connecting the public galleries to conservation labs and storage areas. Sarah heard rapid footsteps behind her- they'd gotten through the staff door quicker than she'd expected. These weren't ordinary security men.

She took a sharp right, then left and headed for the old Victorian service tunnels that ran beneath the museum. Her phone buzzed- a text from James: 'On my way now to Cambridge. King's College Chapel. M has arranged transport'.

The footsteps were getting closer. Sarah reached the basement level, where the museum's oldest foundations met modern construction. Ahead laid an access point to more of London's vast network of underground tunnels- maintenance shafts, old bomb shelters and forgotten passages that connected the city's oldest buildings.

A shout echoed behind her: "Dr. Chen! Stop! We only want to talk!"

Sarah had no intention of stopping. She swiped her access card and slipped through a heavy security door, emerging into a brick-lined tunnel that predated the museum itself. The air was cool and damp, carrying the scent of centuries.

Her phone buzzed again. Malcolm this time: 'Three heading your way through the main tunnel. Fourth circling to Russell Square tube station. I've got eyes on the CCTV. Head for the World War II shelter junction'.

Sarah smiled grimly. Of course, Malcolm was watching. She turned down a narrower passage, one she'd discovered during her research into London's wartime archaeology. The brick walls here showed signs of hasty wartime construction, telling a story of Londoners seeking shelter from the Blitz.

Just behind her, their torchlight bounced off the walls. They were getting closer. Sarah reached the junction Malcolm had mentioned- a spot where wartime tunnels intersected with even older passages. She pressed herself into an alcove, holding her breath as footsteps approached.

"She must have gone toward Russell Square", one voice said. American accent, military precision.

"Split up", another ordered. "Paolo, take the west tunnel. Marco, east. I'll head for the tube station".

Sarah waited until their footsteps faded, then slipped out of her hiding place. Instead of following any of the main tunnels, she located a maintenance shaft she'd also discovered in her archaeological surveys. It would be tight, but it led to something the Vatican team wouldn't expect- the remains of a medieval priory cellar that now connected to the London Underground.

Her phone vibrated: 'They're coordinating with a team above ground', Malcolm warned. 'Tube station exits are being watched. But I've arranged a small distraction'.

Sarah emerged into the abandoned cellar just as a massive power surge hit the Underground's Northern Line. Emergency lighting kicked in and she heard the distant sound of confused passengers being evacuated from Russell Square tube station.

"Thanks, Malcolm", she whispered, using the chaos to slip onto the crowded platform. In the emergency lighting, no one noticed another confused commuter joining the evacuation.

She followed the crowd up to street level, buying precious minutes as Luca's team searched the tunnels below. But she couldn't risk the streets for long- too many CCTV cameras, too many watchers.

Her phone buzzed one last time: 'Package waiting at Postman's Park. Five minutes'.

Sarah knew the place- a hidden Victorian garden near St. Paul's Cathedral, dedicated to ordinary people who died saving others.

The sort of spot tourists rarely found. Perfect.

She moved through London's morning crowds, using every trick she'd learned from years of navigating the city's rush hour. When one of Luca's men appeared at the end of a street, she ducked into a coffee shop, emerging through its back door into an alley she knew connected to the old Roman wall line.

Postman's Park was quiet when she arrived, its memorial plaques gleaming in the weak morning light. A woman in a red coat sat reading a newspaper, an umbrella and shopping bag at her feet. As Sarah passed, the woman spoke without looking up.

"Dreadful weather we're having".

"Better than the Great Fire of 1666", Sarah replied, using Malcolm's recognition code.

The woman stood, leaving the shopping bag. "Best hurry. Train to Cambridge leaves in twenty minutes".

Inside the bag, Sarah found a change of clothes, a new phone and train tickets. The clothes were exactly her size- Malcolm's attention to detail was impressive.

She changed quickly in a public restroom, stuffing her old clothes in a donation bin. The new outfit made her look like any other business commuter heading out of London for meetings.

The final test came at King's Cross. Sarah spotted two of Luca's men watching the barriers but Malcolm's preparations held. Her new phone's electronic ticket worked perfectly and the men's eyes slid right past her altered appearance.

On the train, Sarah finally allowed herself to breathe. The tablet case containing her notes was still secure against her side. Whatever secrets the letter contained, the Vatican had seriously underestimated how far she would go to uncover them.

The journey to Cambridge passed in tense silence. Sarah used three different cabs after arriving, checking carefully for tails before finally approaching King's College Chapel. Its Gothic spires loomed against the grey Cambridge sky, piercing the morning mist like ancient sentinels. She circled the building twice, using shop windows to check for followers. She'd lost the Cardinal's men in the Underground but something told her they weren't people who gave up easily.

CHAPTER 8: The Guardians of Truth

The Chapel's side door opened at her touch, the ancient wood warm beneath her fingers despite the chill morning air. James stood in the shadows of the vestibule, his academic demeanour back in place, though Sarah noticed he still carried himself with the alertness of a man expecting trouble.

"Anyone follow you?"

"Not that I could spot". Sarah handed him her phone, its screen still displaying the photos she'd taken before the Vatican team confiscated the letter. "They have the original letter".

"They don't know what they have".

James led her past the Chapel's famous windows, their stained glass darkened in the early light. Medieval kings and saints watched their passage, their frozen expressions seeming to hold secrets of their own. He stopped at a particular wooden panel in the wall, its carvings so subtle they were almost invisible.

His fingers found hidden pressure points in the ancient wood. "Caiaphas's allies have spent centuries trying to locate and destroy all evidence of his plan. But they never found our archives because they never understood how we hid them".

The panel slid silently aside, revealing a narrow stone staircase descending into darkness. Cool, ancient air wafted up, carrying the scent of centuries.

"The Guardians have been protecting the truth since the first century", James continued as they descended. Their footsteps echoed off worn stone steps that had felt the passage of countless others before them. "The first Guardians were just very committed believers in Christ's message. But over the centuries, our members have included biblical scholars, historians, archaeologists- people who discovered the evidence and agreed to join the work to preserve it. A small few of us are the descendants of Christ's original eyewitnesses, while others are descendants of those who witnessed the conspiracy unfolding".

Sarah ran her hand along the wall, feeling the smoothness where generations of hidden truth-seekers had made the same journey. "How many of you are there?"

"Enough to maintain the vigil. Not enough to stop what's coming without help". James's voice echoed in the narrow space. "That's why we've been watching you, Sarah. Your work on early Christian manuscripts, your expertise in ancient Aramaic- we knew eventually you'd find something they couldn't explain away".

The staircase opened into a room that took Sarah's breath away. Modern computers and preservation equipment lined the walls but the centre was dominated by an ancient stone table she recognised from her studies of early Christian architecture. The contrast between old and new was even more striking than in the London facility.

"Is that...?"

"A first-century communion table". James activated the room's systems with practised efficiency. Banks of monitors flickered to life, casting blue light across the ancient stone. "Used by one of the original apostolic communities. Before Caiaphas and Paul began changing Christ's message of justice and accountability into something more... manageable".

Sarah moved closer to the table, her trained eye noting details she'd only seen in fragments before. "These markings around the edge- they're not just decorative, are they?"

"They're a message. Similar to what you found in your letter but more detailed. A record of their plan to alter Christianity". James touched one of the symbols, his fingers tracing patterns worn smooth by centuries of secret scholars. "The early believers knew what was happening. They left evidence everywhere they could, hoping someone would eventually find it and expose the truth. Remember, Christianity first arrived in England near the end of the third century".

Footsteps echoed from above- the Cardinal's men had found the Chapel entrance.

"How many more locations like this are there?" Sarah asked, quickly photographing the markings with her phone.

"Enough to prove everything. But the key evidence. ." James glanced at his phone, checking for a message.

The first sounds of drilling came from the ceiling. Dust filtered down from ancient stonework, a visible reminder that their time was running out.

"Time to go?" Sarah guessed, trying to keep her voice steady despite the growing tension.

James nodded, moving to another hidden panel. This one was marked with symbols she recognised from early Christian catacombs but they were subtly different. "Ready to see how deep this conspiracy really goes?"

He pressed a sequence of stones, revealing a narrow passageway. Ancient steps descended into darkness, the air heavy with centuries of secrets. Sarah's torch beam caught glimpses of more symbols carved into the walls, disappearing into the blackness below.

"The original smuggling tunnels", James explained as they hurried down. "The same ones they used to hide evidence of the conspiracy during the Reformation. The network stretches for miles under Cambridge. Medieval builders added to Roman foundations and we've been maintaining them ever since".

Sarah's torch revealed more symbols along the walls, each one different from the last. "These markings- they're a map, aren't they? Showing where other evidence was hidden?"

"The Guardians have spent centuries decoding them. Each location reveals another piece of how they changed Christianity. The trail from here leads to Egypt".

Their footsteps echoed on worn stone as the passage continued deeper beneath Cambridge. The air grew colder, older, carrying scents that reminded Sarah of the tomb excavations she'd worked on in Egypt.

"There's something else". James paused at an intersection, checking his phone's map against symbols carved into the junction. "Father Thomas found proof that Caiaphas kept detailed records of every change they planned. He documented exactly how they would alter Christ's message over generations".

"Generations?" Sarah asked.

"Yes. Generations".

Her torch beam revealed more symbols disappearing into the darkness. Her mind was already cataloguing patterns, seeing how the ancient markings formed a complex navigation system. "Where are those records now?"

"According to Father Thomas, they're hidden in a monastery in Egypt's Eastern Desert. A place that's been forgotten by most of the world- except the Vatican".

A rumble from above sent ancient dust filtering down. The drilling was getting closer.

"That's why they're after Father Thomas", Sarah realised, the pieces falling into place. "He's found Caiaphas's actual planning documents?"

"More than that. How much do you know about the Council of Nicaea?" James asked.

"Enough to know it changed Christianity forever", Sarah answered.

"Well, Father Thomas has found proof that the Council of Nicaea wasn't just about establishing doctrine- it was actually the culmination of Caiaphas's plan. Three centuries of carefully orchestrated changes, all leading to one final manipulation".

The tunnel opened into a larger chamber. Medieval arches soared overhead; their stones carved with more of the ancient symbols. But these were different- more detailed, more urgent. Sarah recognised the architectural elements as being from the same period as King's College Chapel. But these spaces had never appeared in any historical record.

"These were carved during the Reformation", James explained, his torch illuminating elaborate sequences of symbols. "Look at this one". James directed his torch to a particular series of symbols. "It shows how they planned each stage. First, add Paul's writings to create new doctrines. Then, use those doctrines to shift focus from God to Christ. Finally, establish the Trinity to cement the changes".

As Sarah studied the carvings, her expertise in ancient languages allowed her to see patterns others might miss. "They're trying to tell us something specific, aren't they? All this effort to make the truth harder to find with each generation", Sarah murmured, understanding dawning. "Until everyone would forget there had ever been a different message".

The drilling stopped abruptly. Then voices, closer now.

James checked his phone, its blue light casting shadows across his face. "Father

Thomas's last known location was Saint Anthony's Monastery. If he found Caiaphas's records..."

"Then that's where the Vatican team is headed". Sarah photographed the last of the symbols, knowing they might never have another chance to document this chamber. "How do we get to Egypt without being followed?"

"The Guardians have maintained certain connections over the centuries". James moved to what looked like a solid wall, revealing another hidden door. "Including some with Britain's intelligence services".

The door opened to reveal a small chamber containing backpacks, clothes and two diplomatic passports. Modern equipment arranged with military precision, ready for exactly this scenario.

"James", Sarah picked up one of the passports. "What exactly did you do in the Royal Marines?"

That half-smile appeared again but his eyes were serious. "Let's just say I had a very

104

specific skill set that made the Guardians recruit me. The same way they recruited Father Thomas thirty years ago when he first discovered discrepancies in early church documents".

Sarah quickly changed into the clothes provided- practical gear suitable for desert travel. "And the Vatican? How long have they been trying to stop this truth from coming out?"

"Since the beginning. But they've never been this aggressive". James checked his weapon before concealing it in his new outfit. "Something's different this time. Maybe they're afraid".

"Why? Because of digital communication? Global access to information?"

"Partly. But I think it's more than that". He handed her a satellite phone, its weight reassuring in her hand.

More footsteps above, moving with purpose now.

"Time to go?" Sarah asked, though she already knew the answer.

James nodded, securing their evidence in waterproof bags. "The Guardians have a plane waiting at a private airfield. We can be in Egypt by morning".

"Where the real answers are hidden".

"Where everything started". James took her hand and this time the contact felt natural, necessary. "Ready?"

Sarah thought of her quiet life at the museum, of all the years she'd spent studying ancient texts without knowing their true significance. Now, she was about to hunt for evidence of the greatest conspiracy in Christian history.

"Ready".

They slipped through the door just as the first sounds of pursuers echoed in the tunnel behind them. As they hurried through the darkness, Sarah realised this was just the beginning. The real journey- and the real danger- still lay ahead.

But something else had changed too. The way James held her hand, the trust building between them with each revelation and shared danger- it was more than just professional cooperation now. Whatever they found in Egypt's desert monasteries would change more than just religious history.

It would change them too.

The Petrine Promise

CHAPTER 9: The Bermondsey Evidence

The private airfield looked abandoned in the pre-dawn light but Sarah had learned to distrust appearances. Nothing in James's world was quite what it seemed.

"MI6 maintains this facility", he explained as they approached a sleek Cessna Citation. The jet's polished surface reflected the first hints of sunrise, its engines already humming with pre-flight checks. "The Guardians have certain arrangements with them. Mutual interests in preserving historical truth".

Sarah clutched the waterproof bag containing their evidence from Bermondsey, its weight seeming to grow heavier with each step. "And they don't mind us borrowing their jet?"

"As long as we share what we find". James guided her aboard, his hand resting lightly on her lower back. "The intelligence community has its own concerns about Vatican operations on British soil".

The jet's interior was all leather and polished wood but Sarah barely noticed the luxury. As soon as they were airborne, she spread the documents across the small table between them. Her fingers traced the ancient ink of Caiaphas's letters, still perfectly legible after two millennia.

"I still can't believe he documented everything", she said, organising the papers into chronological order. "Why keep such detailed records of a conspiracy?"

"Pride". James settled beside her, close enough that she could feel the warmth of his body. "He wanted future generations of religious leaders to understand how brilliantly he'd managed to change Christianity. Look at this letter to the Jerusalem elders".

Sarah translated the Aramaic text, her voice growing tense as the words revealed their meaning:

"'The Apostles' message spreads too quickly, taking root among both Jews and Gentiles. Their call for justice threatens our authority, their insistence on accountability challenges our position. But I have found the solution. The brilliant young Pharisee, Saul, understands what must be done. Through him, we will create new scriptures, new doctrines. By the time we are finished, no one will remember there was ever a simpler message.'"

"He was right", James said quietly. "For nearly two thousand years, it has worked".

Sarah moved to another document, this one written in a different hand. "This one is from Paul himself: 'The plan proceeds as expected. My letters are being copied, distributed. I write in Greek. They wrote in Aramaic. However, few question my authority, though my doctrines differ from what the Apostles teach. The emphasis on faith alone draws attention away from their inconvenient message of faith *and* works...'"

The jet's engines hummed steadily as they examined more evidence. Letters, meeting records, carefully planned strategies for altering Christian doctrine over generations.

James's phone buzzed- a message from his Guardian contacts. "Vatican team spotted boarding a flight to Cairo. They're following the same trail".

"At least we know we're on the right track". As Sarah started carefully repacking the documents, her hands lingered on the ancient papers.

"James- do you remember when we were back in the safe house and I said- it wasn't just about modifying the original message- it was actually about erasing the evidence that a different message had ever existed?" James nodded. "Well, we can prove this now. Have you ever heard about the Grigory Kessel discovery?" Sarah asked.

"Yes", James replied. "There were articles about him everywhere two years ago. But not so much now. From publications like the 'New York Post' to very respected academic journals like the 'New Testament Studies'. Why do you ask?"

Sarah's face lit up. "His discovery has been my pet project for the past two years. And frankly, I've been surprised that there wasn't more reaction in the scientific community to the implications of his discovery. But now I get it. Together with what we now know, the only possible explanation for his discovery is that it proves that there was a deliberate effort to literally erase out of existence the apostolic testimonies".

Sarah paused for a minute and then continued. "The conventional explanation for what Kessel discovered. What we call- the Syriac undertexts- is that writing materials were scarce in the first millennium and were, therefore, re-used by different authors over time. They washed the writing materials or literally scraped off one set of text so that they could write something new on top.

"But if that were true and the Greek Bible had come first, then the Greek writing should be the undertext and not the other way around! The Apostles Aramaic writing is the undertext. This proves that it was written first…"

James smiled as he looked at Sarah. "Your mystery is solved. Caiaphas and Paul never thought that a technology would develop that allows us to expose their conspiracy.

113

I'm sure you know that the 1,750-year-old Greek Bible manuscript that had the Kessel text was just one of many documents secured in St. Catherine's Monastery.

"It is a monastery that's at the foot of Mount Sinai (in the Sinai Peninsula of Egypt)- where God engraved the tablets with the Ten Commandments. It is also the site of the burning bush that didn't get consumed. The one that Moses came to see- near Mount Horeb. The bush is protected within the Monastery's walls. The Codex Sinaiticus and the Syriac Sinaiticus biblical manuscripts were also both found at this Monastery. The only place that holds a larger collection of biblical manuscripts than St. Catherine's is the Vatican Library.

"We weren't surprised by Kessel's discovery- it just confirmed the other evidence that the Guardians have already collected proving the Caiaphas conspiracy".

The two sat quietly for a while, each deep in their own thoughts. Sarah broke the silence first. "But James, something's bothering me. All this evidence of the conspiracy is crucial but what exactly did Father Thomas find in Egypt? What has made the Vatican suddenly move against him now?"

"According to our sources, he found Caiaphas's personal journal, which detailed the final manipulation. Remember what the Yair Letter mentioned? And not just records of what they planned to do but why. The real reason they needed to change Christ's message".

"And that reason was?"

James's expression was grim in the cabin's dim light. "That's what we need to find out. But based on these documents, it was about more than just protecting their religious authority. Something in Christ's original message threatened the entire power structure of the ancient world".

"And still threatens power structures today", Sarah added, understanding dawning. "That's why they're so desperate to stop us…"

"Exactly. Which is why we need to protect that journal". James checked their flight path on a tablet. "Two more hours to Cairo. Then we follow Father Thomas's trail to Saint Anthony's".

Sarah studied the Bermondsey evidence and the Cambridge photos one more time, her eyes taking in details she'd missed before. "All these centuries of deception, of deliberately hiding the truth. How did they think they'd get away with it forever?"

"As I said- they didn't expect technology. Instant global communication with the ability to share discoveries worldwide instantly, digital scanning and digital preservation". James smiled, reaching out to tuck a strand of hair behind her ear. The casual intimacy of the gesture made her catch her breath. "And they definitely didn't expect you to find that letter".

"Just doing my job. Though I didn't expect it to lead to a secret society, a historic conspiracy and a midnight flight to Egypt". She tried to keep her voice light but the weight of what they'd discovered pressed in on her.

"Having second thoughts?"

116

Sarah thought of the letter that had started everything, of Christ's original message waiting to be rediscovered. Of the way James looked at her now, like she was something precious and dangerous all at once. "No. The world needs to know the truth".

"Even if it changes everything?"

"Especially if it changes everything".

The desert dawn was breaking outside their window, painting the sky in shades of gold and rose. Somewhere ahead lay Saint Anthony's Monastery and the answers they sought. But Sarah had a feeling their Bermondsey evidence was just the beginning.

She glanced at James, noting how the rising sun turned his profile to bronze. The scholar she'd argued with over coffee had become something more- partner, protector, possibly something else she wasn't ready to name yet. Whatever awaited them in Egypt's ancient deserts, at least they would face it together.

The real revelations- and the real danger-
was waiting for them in Egypt. But for now,
in the quiet of the cabin, with evidence of
history's greatest conspiracy spread between
them, Sarah allowed herself to feel
something like peace.

It wouldn't last, she knew. The Vatican teams
would be waiting. They didn't know exactly
where Father Thomas was. And somewhere
in those desert monasteries lay the truth
about why Christianity had been changed- a
truth some would kill to keep hidden.

They had some evidence. They had each
other. And soon, they would have answers to
questions that had been buried for two
thousand years.

The desert sun climbed higher as their jet
raced east, carrying them towards destiny.
Or to doom. Only time would tell which.

CHAPTER 10: The Road to Nicaea

Cairo's morning heat hit them like a wall as they descended from the plane. The city sprawled beneath a haze of dust and diesel fumes, ancient minarets piercing a sky the colour of beaten brass. A Guardian contact- a lean, weathered man who introduced himself only as Ahmed- waited with a rugged Land Rover.

"Father Thomas's last known location was the Monastery library", he told them as they loaded their gear. "But he wasn't alone. Vatican agents arrived shortly after".

"And now?" James asked, his hand lingering near the weapon concealed beneath his jacket.

"No sign of him. But there's been unusual activity at several desert monasteries. The Coptic priests are nervous". Ahmed's dark eyes scanned the parking area. "Something's stirring that hasn't stirred in centuries".

Sarah studied the map Ahmed provided. Saint Anthony's Monastery lay a six-hour drive east, nestled against the Red Sea mountains. It is the oldest Christian monastery in the world- its construction started in 298 AD and was completed in 356 AD.

"What exactly did Father Thomas tell you he was looking for?" Sarah asked.

"Records from Nicaea. But not the official ones". Ahmed navigated through Cairo's chaotic traffic with the skill of someone who'd done it for decades. "He said he's found evidence that the Coptic churches kept their own accounts of the Council of Nicaea meeting. What really happened there".

The city gave way to desert, ancient and unforgiving. Sarah reviewed their evidence as they drove, looking for connections.

When he was sure that they weren't being followed, Ahmed reached under his car seat to retrieve a package. "Father Thomas told me to give this parcel to you. In case he didn't make it out..." He handed Sarah a rumpled brown paper bag with a few scrolls inside.

She started to translate:

"Here's a letter dated just before the Council of Nicaea meeting: 'Everything is prepared. The bishops who might oppose our changes have been carefully identified. Some will be delayed on their journeys. Others will find their invitations mysteriously lost. Only those who understand the importance of our work will have a significant voice.'"

"They stacked the Council", James noted. "Ensuring they'd get the result Caiaphas had planned for, centuries before".

"But the Coptic churches knew". Sarah held up another document. "This warns about 'brothers in Egypt who kept their own records, who remembered the original teachings.' No wonder the Vatican's worried about what Father Thomas found".

The desert sun climbed higher as Ahmed pushed the Land Rover faster. James received regular updates on his phone-Vatican teams moving through the desert, satellite imagery showing vehicles converging on the monastery.

Suddenly, Ahmed slowed, pulling off the main road onto a barely visible track. "We take the old pilgrim route from here. The one they used in Nicaea's time".

The track wound through ancient wadis, dry riverbeds that had guided travellers for millennia. Sarah gasped as they rounded a bend- ahead lay the ruins of a way station, its mud-brick walls still bearing traces of early Christian symbols.

"A rest stop for bishops travelling to Nicaea", Ahmed explained. "Some never made it past here. The ones who opposed Caiaphas' plans had unfortunate... accidents".

James pointed at the weathered walls. "Look at those markings- they're the same symbols we found in Cambridge".

Sarah nodded. "They're telling a story. About bishops who knew what was coming. Who tried to preserve evidence of the truth".

A distant engine sound made them all freeze.

"Vatican teams", Ahmed said grimly. "They're searching every historical site along the route".

They pressed on, the Land Rover bouncing over terrain that hadn't changed since Roman times. As they drove, Ahmed spoke of the desert's secrets- of monks who'd fled here after Nicaea, preserving texts that contradicted the official doctrine.

"The desert preserves things", he said. "Papers, yes, but also truths. Memories. The Coptic Church remembers what others tried to get their true believers to forget".

The Monastery appeared suddenly- ancient walls rising from red mountains like a fortress against time itself. But something was wrong. Even from a distance, they could see there was too much activity, too many vehicles.

"We're too late", Ahmed said quietly. "They're already here".

James studied the scene through binoculars. "Multiple teams. Armed. Professional. They're conducting a systematic search".

"For what?" Sarah asked.

"According to my sources, there's a sealed chamber beneath the Monastery's original church. Father Thomas believed that's where the Coptic priests hid their records of Nicaea".

"Can we get inside?"

Ahmed smiled for the first time. "The Vatican may know about the chamber. But they don't know about the cave system that connects to it. The desert monks have kept that secret for centuries".

They waited until dark before approaching the Monastery. Ahmed led them through narrow canyons to a hidden entrance- steps carved into living rock, descending into darkness.

"The original hermit caves", he explained. "They run for miles under the mountains. The monks adapted them over centuries, creating hidden chambers for exactly this purpose- protecting evidence of the truth".

Their torchlight revealed more ancient symbols carved into the rock walls- the same ones they'd seen in Cambridge. Sarah traced them with her fingers.

"They're like chapters in a book", she said. "Each location reveals another piece of how they changed Christianity. How they suppressed Christ's message".

The passage opened into a small chamber. Ancient oil lamps still sat in wall niches, waiting to be lit. But it was the far wall that caught their attention- covered in detailed carvings that made Sarah catch her breath.

"It's a record of Nicaea", she whispered. "Day by day, decision by decision. Everything that wasn't included in the official accounts".

James began photographing the wall while Sarah translated:

"'They came prepared, knowing what must be done. Each vote carefully orchestrated; each decision followed the plan laid down centuries before. The Trinity doctrine, making Christ equal to God. Salvation through faith alone, removing the requirement for works of justice. One by one, the Apostles' original teachings were buried beneath new doctrines..."'

A sound echoed from the passage- voices, footsteps.

"They've found the cave entrance", Ahmed warned.

"Wait". Sarah's torch had revealed something else- a small alcove, hidden behind an oil lamp shelf. Inside lay a leather case, old but well-preserved.

James reached it first. "Father Thomas was here. This is his research kit".

"How clever of him to leave it behind!" Sarah exclaimed. "Even if the Vatican teams had managed to find him, they still wouldn't have captured the evidence that he found. And if we hadn't found it, no doubt, the Coptic monks would have continued protecting it".

Inside the case, they found his notes and beneath them, something that made Sarah's heart race- a scroll sealed with an imperial Roman seal.

"Read it", James urged as Ahmed kept watch.

Sarah's fingers trembled as she carefully unrolled the ancient parchment. "This is... this is a letter from Senator Claudius Silvanus to Caiaphas. From the date, it looks like it was written before Paul's so-called conversion". Her voice grew tight with tension as she translated:

"'The situation becomes untenable. This new sect spreads dangerous ideas- equality between men and women, acceptance of all peoples, judgment based on actions. Worse still, they even insist that slaves and commoners have worth equal to nobles. You know what Constantine requires- a religion that unifies the empire while maintaining proper order. See to it. One of your Pharisees- the one called Saul of Tarsus- shows promise for our purposes. He is quite aggressive and shows a natural dislike for the Christians. We will send a scribe from Rome- Tertius- to befriend him and guide Saul's writing. Tertius knows what we want. Your orders are to ensure that Tertius's writings get included with those of the direct witnesses.'"

"Political manipulation from the very beginning", James said softly.

For a moment, Sarah stopped translating and looked at James. "Oh my gosh, biblical scholars always dismissed the 'Tertius Admission' of Romans 16:22! But this Silvanus letter proves Paul's letter to the Romans was written by the Roman scribe Tertius".

"It seems so", James replied. An air of disbelief mixed with anger had entered the group. "You are aware- Paul never refuted Tertius's claim of authorship of the epistle to the Romans". James paused to listen for signs of followers.

Hearing nothing, he continued. "And, for further proof of his Roman connections, in the very next verse, Tertius goes on to mention the Roman men that he spent time with- his Roman host and landlord Gaius and his good friend Erastus, the Roman City Treasurer. Do we know why Tertius provided details about these historical relationships? No, we don't---"

"So", Sarah interjected. "The book that Paul is most famous for- Romans, was actually written by a Roman scribe in furtherance of the Silvanus-Caiaphas-Paul conspiracy?"

"That's right, Sarah. Biblical scholars have always dismissed the significance of the Romans 16:22-23 verses and we've never had proof of anything untoward until now. The Romans saw the threat in Christ's original message and wanted to ensure they controlled its replacement message completely. By using Tertius, they ensured they had this control- to the word and to the letter!"

Sarah went back to her translating:

"'We cannot allow this message of universal justice to spread. Create new doctrines. Focus their attention on the afterlife rather than on earthly conditions. Make them pray for their oppressors rather than seek change. The stability of the empire depends on it.'"

A crash echoed from above- the Vatican teams were breaking into the Monastery proper.

"There's more", Sarah said, her torch revealing another chamber. "Letters from bishops who tried to resist at Nicaea. The records about those who disappeared on their way to the Council".

Ahmed's voice was urgent. "If we're going to get out of here alive, we have to get going now!"

They moved deeper into the cave system. Ancient passages twisted through the mountain's heart, each turn revealing more evidence- more symbols, more hidden caches of documents. Sarah's trained eye caught patterns in the markings.

"These aren't just direction markers", she realised. "They're telling us where to look. See this symbol? It's the same one that was on Caiaphas's seal".

The passage opened into a larger chamber, its walls lined with more niches cut into the living rock. Each niche held clay jars, sealed and numbered in the ancient Coptic script.

"The complete record", Ahmed breathed. "Everything the desert fathers preserved about Nicaea and what came before".

James was already examining the jars. "Look at these dates- some go back to Paul's time. Letters, meeting records, everything they planned..."

A voice echoed down the passage- Cardinal Romano's distinctive tone: "Dr. Chen? Dr. Bradford? We know you're down there. Let's discuss this like reasonable people".

Sarah's fingers flew across the ancient pottery, searching for specific dates. "Here- this one's marked with the year of Nicaea".

"'The plan proceeds as expected'", Sarah translated quickly. "'The bishops are chosen, the votes secured. When Nicaea concludes, no one will remember there was ever a different Christianity. The empire will have its unified religion and the old message of justice will be forever...'"

Footsteps approached. Too close.

"Time to go", James said, carefully repacking the documents. "Ahmed?"

The Egyptian guide pressed a series of carved symbols on the wall. A section of rock shifted, revealing another passage. "The old escape route. It leads to---"

The rat-tat-tat of bullets sparked off the wall near his head.

"Run!" James returned fire, covering their retreat. "Sarah- don't wait for me! If we get separated, get those documents to safety!"

Sarah and Ahmed fled deeper into the mountain's heart, pursued by Vatican agents and their own echoing footsteps. Sarah clutched the precious documents, knowing they were carrying proof of something much bigger than they'd ever imagined- evidence that the transformation of Christianity had been executed by Caiaphas but ordered by the highest levels of Roman power.

And somewhere lay the final proof- the discovery that would reveal why an ancient political conspiracy still mattered today. And why, after two thousand years, powerful people still feared its rediscovery.

The chase was no longer just about ancient documents. It was about a truth that could shake the foundations of modern power structures.

The Petrine Promise

CHAPTER 11: Coptic Secrets

The desert night had spread like black velvet above them as Sarah and Ahmed ran out from the mountain tunnels. Stars sparkled overhead. They were unchanged since the days when the first monks had hidden their precious documents in St. Anthony's chambers. Sarah clutched Father Thomas's leather case with its cache of rescued documents, her heart still racing from their escape.

"Three vehicles heading north on the main road", Ahmed reported, checking his phone. "They think we're trying to reach Cairo".

Ahmed guided her along a narrow track that seemed to disappear into the darkness. "But they don't know about the old pilgrim routes". His voice carried the satisfaction of someone who'd lived for this exact moment. "Or the airfield hidden in the wadi".

Sarah's trained eye caught the remnants of ancient way-markers as they moved through the darkness- the same symbols they'd seen in the Monastery's tunnels. "These paths", she breathed. "They're from the earliest days, aren't they? When the desert fathers were first preserving the evidence".

"The same routes they used to share messages between monasteries", Ahmed confirmed. "While Nicaea's changes were being forced on the rest of Christianity, the desert preserved the truth".

Their vehicle was waiting exactly where Ahmed had hidden it and covered it in desert camouflage, making it nearly invisible in the starlight. As Ahmed began removing the camouflage, James stepped out from the darkness. "We weren't followed", he said.

Sarah let out a small scream. "Don't do that! You really scared me. How did you get here before us?"

"Malcolm". James answered as he stepped forward to help Ahmed remove the camouflage covering the Land Rover.

"Well, I'm glad you survived Dr. Bradford". Sarah was still upset that she had been frightened by his appearance.

"Are we back to Dr. Bradford and Dr. Chen?" James said quietly as he walked over to her and looked into her eyes intently.

She couldn't tell what he was thinking but she knew she was blushing. She turned away and started examining the documents in her arms.

"I found a letter", she said, her torch revealing ancient Coptic script. "From one desert monastery to another. Listen to this: 'They have begun implementing the changes in the cities. Paul's writings are being elevated above the Apostles' testimonies. But we maintain the original collection. We remember what Christianity was before they changed it...'"

A distant engine sound made them all freeze.

"Time to go", James said, helping her into the vehicle. "We can examine everything properly once we're airborne".

They drove in tense silence, Ahmed navigating by memory through wadis that hadn't changed since Roman times. The stars were beginning to fade, first light was threatening in the east, when they reached the hidden airfield. It was little more than a strip of packed sand marked by ancient stones.

A sleek aircraft waited, its engines already idling. Malcolm's arrangements, Sarah guessed. The Guardian's technical genius seemed to think of everything.

"Ahmed", James turned to their guide as they finished loading the bags. "You're sure you won't come with us?"

The Egyptian smiled, a smile that crinkled his eyes and bared his teeth. "My place is here, protecting what remains in the desert. But you have my number if you need my help- when you find the next piece of the puzzle".

"The next piece?" Sarah asked.

"The Coptic Pope's archive in Alexandria", Ahmed said. "What you've found here is just the beginning. The desert preserved the truth, yes. But Alexandria? Alexandria documented everything. Every change they made to the doctrine, every bishop who opposed them..."

A glint of light on the horizon- vehicle headlamps.

"Go", Ahmed urged. "Before they realise this airstrip exists".

As they climbed aboard, Sarah caught one last glimpse of their guide melting into the desert shadows, as though the landscape itself was protecting him. Then they were airborne, the rising sun painting the mountains gold beneath them.

"Sarah", James's voice drew her attention back to their precious cargo. "Let's see what we found".

She carefully began laying out documents on the small table in front of them, her training in antiquities taking over. "We'll need to catalogue everything systematically. Cross-reference any dates or names..."

"Start with that one", James pointed to a particular scroll- its case marked with symbols she recognised from the

Monastery's walls. "Ahmed's reaction when we found it suggested it was significant".

Sarah carefully unrolled the ancient parchment. "It's... it's a record of a secret meeting. Just before Nicaea. Listen:

'We, the undersigned, gather to preserve testimony of what we have witnessed. They are changing the doctrine, piece by piece. First, they elevated Paul's writings to equal standing with the Apostles' testimonies. Now they prepare to alter our understanding of God Himself...'"

James leaned closer, his shoulder brushing hers. "The Trinity doctrine?"

Sarah nodded, continuing to translate: "'They will declare Christ equal to the Father, though He Himself said 'my Father is greater than I.' They will make salvation a matter of faith alone, though our Lord taught that we would be judged by our works. They will build hierarchies of authority, though Jesus showed us a better way...'"

"This proves it was deliberate", James said softly. "Not just theological evolution but carefully planned changes".

"There's more", Sarah said as her fingers traced the ancient text. "'But we have preserved the original records- the true testimonies of those who walked with Christ. Records that show Christianity as it was meant to be. While they build their new doctrine in the cities, we of the desert will maintain the truth...'"

The jet's engines hummed steadily as they worked through more documents. Letters between monasteries. Records of secret meetings. Lists of changes being implemented in the major Christian centres. All pointing to a systematic transformation of Christ's message.

"James", Sarah held up another scroll. "This one's different. It's from Alexandria, talking about their own archives: 'We have documented everything. Every change, every protest, every bishop who tried to resist. When the time comes for truth to be revealed, the evidence will be waiting...'"

A memory tickled at her mind. "The Alexandrian church was already ancient when St. Anthony's was founded, wasn't it? The tradition says Mark himself established it..."

"Yes", James answered. "How ironic it is that right under the nose of one of Paul's primary associates, in the church that he established, monks dedicated to the truth were able to hide evidence of Caiaphas' conspiracy. And they seem to have kept incredibly detailed records of everything..."

The airplane's phone rang- it was Malcolm: "Vatican teams regrouping in Cairo. Chatter suggests they know about Alexandria".

"They're figuring it out", James said grimly. "Following the same trail we are".

Sarah looked at the evidence spread before them- proof of deliberate changes to doctrine but hints of something deeper still waiting to be found. "How long until we reach Alexandria?"

"Forty minutes". James began carefully repacking their documents. "But we'll need a plan. The Vatican teams won't make the same mistake twice. They won't assume we've fled- they'll be waiting for us".

"Then we better hope the Guardians have friends in Alexandria too".

James smiled at her. "As it happens, I know a certain Coptic priest who's been waiting years for someone to come asking the right questions".

Sarah glanced out the window. The Mediterranean glittered ahead, past Cairo's sprawl. Somewhere in that ancient port city, more evidence waited. Proof of exactly how they'd changed Christianity, piece by deliberate piece.

They just had to reach it first.

The race wasn't over. In many ways, it was just beginning.

The Petrine Promise

CHAPTER 12: The Alexandria Letters

Alexandria's ancient harbour stretched before them, a crescent of blue water holding twenty centuries of secrets. Their small boat, arranged by James's Coptic contact, wove between larger vessels toward a section of waterfront that looked forgotten by time.

"The original Christian quarter", James explained as they approached a weathered dock. "Two thousand years ago, this was the centre of everything".

"Before they built the great library?" Sarah asked, her historian's mind already mapping the layers of history.

"Before all of it". James's eyes scanned the waterfront. No sign of Vatican teams yet but that couldn't last. "The Coptic church kept their own archives separate from the famous library. A good thing, too- when the library burned, their records survived".

A figure waited in the shadow of an ancient archway- elderly, wearing the simple black robes of a Coptic priest. As they tied up at the dock, Sarah noticed subtle symbols carved into the stonework above him- the same marks they'd seen in the desert.

"Father Mikhail", James said as they approached. "Thank you for meeting us".

"The Guardians have been good friends to us". The priest's English carried the lilt of someone who'd studied at Oxford. "And now that you've found the desert evidence..." His eyes fixed on Sarah's backpack. "Perhaps it's time for you to see what Alexandria preserved".

He led them through narrow streets that seemed unchanged since Roman times. Ancient churches and monasteries rose on all sides, their walls holding centuries of prayers. Finally, they reached a courtyard dominated by a church whose architecture spoke of extreme age.

"The original archive was destroyed in the ninth century", Father Mikhail explained as he unlocked a heavy wooden door. "But not before everything important was moved here. We've been adding to the collection ever since- every scrap of evidence about how they changed our Lord's message".

The door opened to reveal a steep staircase descending into darkness. As they followed the priest down, Sarah's torch caught glimpses of more ancient symbols on the walls- but these were different from the ones in the desert. More detailed. More urgent.

"Warning marks", Father Mikhail said, noting her interest. "When they began changing the doctrine, our forebears developed a whole language of symbols. Different marks for distinct types of changes they were making. The desert preserved the truth- but Alexandria documented the lies".

The staircase ended in a chamber that took Sarah's breath away. Floor-to-ceiling shelves lined with ancient codices. Glass cases protecting fragile scrolls. And at the centre, another massive stone table whose surface was covered in the same symbolic language they'd seen on the walls.

"A map", the priest explained. "Showing every major centre where they implemented the changes. Every place where they suppressed the original message. And here..." He pointed to Alexandria's position on the map. "Every piece of evidence we collected".

Sarah moved to examine the nearest shelf, her trained eye noting the organisation system. "Are these arranged chronologically?"

"Yes. By year, then by location. We documented everything- letters between bishops discussing the changes, records of meetings where they planned new doctrines, lists of those who opposed them..."

"And those who disappeared", James added grimly, studying a particular section of the map.

Father Mikhail nodded. "The cost of resistance was high. But still, they kept records. Still, they preserved evidence of what Christianity had been- and what it became".

Sarah scanned the array of records. "Where should we start?"

"Here". The priest moved to a specific shelf, his hands working quickly as footsteps echoed faintly above them. He carefully removed a bound collection of papyri. "Evidence of when they first elevated Paul's writings".

Sarah scanned the ancient text, translating key passages: "'They claim new authority for Saul's letters... salvation through faith alone, though Christ taught us our works reveal true belief... hierarchies of power, though Jesus showed a different way---'"

A loud crash from above cut her short.

"They're searching the sanctuary", Father Mikhail whispered. "We must hurry".

A distant sound made them all look up-footsteps in the church above.

"The morning service", Father Mikhail said but James was already moving to check.

"No". His voice was tight. "Vatican teams. They've found us".

Sarah's hands moved quickly but carefully, photographing documents while Father Mikhail and James gathered the most crucial evidence. The footsteps were getting closer.

"This way". The priest pressed a section of wall, revealing another staircase. "The original escape route, from the days of Roman persecution. It leads to---"

"Father Mikhail". Cardinal Romano's distinctive voice called out. "We know you're down there. Let's discuss this reasonably".

The priest's face hardened. "Go. There are things they must not find. When you reach the harbour, ask for Youssef at the Blue Door. He'll know what to do next".

"What about you?" Sarah asked.

"My place is here, protecting what remains. Now go- there's one more piece of evidence you must find. The final proof is hidden in Jerusalem..."

The hidden door closed behind them just as torchlight flooded the archive chamber. As they hurried through ancient tunnels, Sarah could hear Father Mikhail's voice raised in argument with the Cardinal.

"James", she clutched their precious evidence. "What's in Jerusalem? What final proof?"

"According to Guardian records, Joseph of Arimathea didn't just provide his tomb for Christ's burial. He also provided a secure location for preserving the Apostles' original manuscripts and other documents. If we can find it..."

More footsteps echoed through the tunnels- Vatican teams had found this escape route too.

"If we can find it", Sarah finished, "we'll have irrefutable proof of exactly what Christianity was meant to be".

They emerged into sunlight near the harbour, the Mediterranean's blue waters beckoning with escape. But Sarah knew they couldn't run forever. Somewhere in Jerusalem, the final piece of evidence waited- proof that would validate everything they'd discovered.

They just had to outsmart Cardinal Romano's men and stay alive long enough to reach Jerusalem first.

CHAPTER 13: Star Light, Star Bright

Their boat bobbed gently in the water. Sunset had come and gone. Now, the sky was dark and filled with glittering stars.

Malcolm had contacted James and warned him not to go to the airport for their flight to Jerusalem. There were too many Vatican agents waiting for them there.

Youssef had picked up some bread, wine and cheese for them. It was basic but at least they would not go hungry. On any other occasion, James mused- sleeping on a boat, under the stars, with a beautiful woman and a bottle of wine would have been very romantic. But there was no time for romantic complications. More than ever, he needed to keep his head clear right now. He glanced over at Sarah. She was looking at the stars intently.

"Are you looking for an answer to one of life's big unanswered questions?" he asked.

Sarah smiled. "No. Nothing so philosophical. I'm just trying to sort out

what we know and what we don't know, at
this point".

"Good idea", James said, as he smiled back
at her. "You start from the beginning while I
pour us some wine".

"Ok. First, there was the Yair Letter
discovery. This alerted *me* to the Caiaphas
conspiracy, which you, apparently, already
knew all about!" Sarah laughed softly as she
looked at James.

James jumped in. "True. Don't forget to
include what we learned from this letter
fragment. It was written in Aramaic. Yair
claimed to be an eyewitness of the
conspiracy. The conspiracy involved two
inter-connected things. First- adding non-
commissioned writings to the New
Testament. Second- these new writings had
to change Christ's core message".

"Yes. You're right", Sarah continued. "At
the 'Heart', I saw authenticated copies of
correspondence between Caiaphas and Paul
and other incriminating documents, which
confirmed what the Yair Letter had
claimed".

"In Cambridge", Sarah continued, "in the Guardians' repository underneath the Anglican Chapel, I saw evidence that ordinary believers had left clues about what they were witnessing- the alterations in Christ's message. But somehow, their efforts to raise an alarm never bore fruit. They always got stopped".

Sarah stopped abruptly. "By the way, I forgot to include that the Vatican's Cardinal Romano took the Yair Letter and his agents have been following us ever since then".

"Yes. Let's not forget that", James snarled. The mood on the boat had shifted.

After a few minutes had passed, Sarah sighed. "Let's continue. Doing this summary is a good idea. It will help keep us focused when we arrive in Jerusalem tomorrow".

"You're right, Sarah. Please continue".

Sarah started again. "During the flight to Egypt, we discovered three more pieces of the puzzle. First- another look at the Bermondsey evidence from the 'Heart' confirmed that Caiaphas had actively recruited Saul. Second- we realised that Grigory Kessel's 2023 discovery of Syriac undertexts supports the accusation of a New Testament canon conspiracy. Third- you got word that Father Thomas's discovery in the Monastery in Egypt would help us identify the 'final manipulation'".

Sarah stopped to take a sip of her wine. "Hmm. This is really nice red wine. Full-bodied. Dry. Just the way I like it. Is it just me or does running for your life as you uncover the biggest conspiracy in history make wine taste better?" They both burst out in muffled laughter.

"Shhh, Sarah. We can't afford to get caught now. Obviously, Cardinal Romano's men have realised that we're not coming to the airport tonight. But they may decide to backtrack and look for us here".

"You're right. But you have to agree", Sarah paused and then added quietly, "if we make it out of here alive, no glass of wine will ever taste as good as this one does tonight". They lifted their glasses to the evening sky in a silent toast and offered a prayer for survival.

The silence under the stars was calming. The boat continued to bob gently from side to side. "Have you finished with your summing up?" James asked.

"No, not yet". Sarah resumed her summary. "At the caves of St. Anthony's Monastery, we discovered two more important things. First- Caiaphas' final manipulation was to subvert the Council of Nicaea, held in 325AD. History has reported that this Council was in complete agreement in approving the Trinity doctrine and the salvation by faith alone doctrine. But now we know, this was not true. Second- we discovered that Caiaphas was not acting alone. He was taking instructions from Rome. We got the scroll that Senator Claudius Silvanus had sent to Caiaphas instructing him to recruit Saul and introduce new writings into the New Testament".

"Ah, yes", said James softly. "It wasn't just a religious conspiracy. It was a political conspiracy, too. Even I didn't know that factoid before".

"Neither did I", Sarah replied. "And let's not forget that the *supposed* foundational text of the New Testament- The Epistle to the Romans- was, in fact, written by a Roman Scribe named Tertius!"

"And this was arranged by Senator Silvanus himself!" James added, sarcastically.

"Sarah- are you finished now?"

"No. But I'm almost finished". Sarah continued with her summing up. "Through Father Mikhail, the Coptic Priest, we got evidence that there was strong dissent at the Nicaea meeting to the direction Paul's writings were pulling the Church towards. So, in the end, it appears they hadn't been able to prevent all the no-voters from attending the Council. But funny, history doesn't report the magnitude of this dissension either. Also, we found out that our next stop would be the Tomb of Joseph of Arimathaea. The original Apostolic manuscripts, written in Aramaic, are supposed to be hidden there. This is proof that all the supposed 'first' Bibles written in Greek actually came after the apostolic manuscripts".

Sarah finished her wine and laid back to look up to the night sky. A long-forgotten phrase from a nursery rhyme popped into her head- '*Star Light, Star Bright*'.

What were the words to that nursery rhyme, Sarah pondered as she gazed at the night sky.

"James", Sarah turned towards him to ask his help. *He seems to know everything*, she thought. "Do you remember a nursery rhyme that has the words: 'star light, star bright' in it?"

"Seriously?" James looked at Sarah and shook his head. With a chuckle in his voice, he said "Sarah, you never fail to amaze me. Let me see, I have to go back a few decades into my memory bank".

He was quiet for a while and then said, "Got it! My grandmother used to read nursery rhymes to me to get me to sleep. I think it goes:

'Star light, star bright,
First star I see tonight,
I wish I may, I wish I might,
Have this wish I wish tonight'.

Is that the nursery rhyme you're thinking of?"

Sarah nodded yes but didn't speak. A peaceful silence fell over them as they bobbed in the harbour's waters.

"Your turn", Sarah murmured, eventually. "I did the 'what we know' part. You have to do the 'what we don't know' part". At last, precious sleep was finally coming. "But keep it short. I'm ready to fall asleep".

James smiled. "Ok. I'll keep it short. Three 'what we don't knows'. Number 1- Why is the Vatican fighting so hard to stop us from finding out the truth? Number 2- If some of the Guardians are descendants of eyewitnesses to the truth, does that mean some of the people who carried forward Caiaphas's plans, through the centuries, were his descendants or descendants of his allies? Or is there something deeper and wildly prophetic behind their willingness to hide the truth? Number 3- What are we planning to do with all the evidence we've discovered? Are we really planning to tell the world that what they thought they knew about Christianity was just a made-up story mixed in with Christ's real message? And if we do that, do we know how the world will react? Will it make even more people abandon Christianity or will it help to invigorate the followers of the true faith?"

Sarah sat up. All sleep was suddenly gone. They looked at each other but neither said a word.

What would tomorrow bring? Neither of them knew. But they had to keep going. They were too close to the truth to stop now.

The Petrine Promise

CHAPTER 14: Hidden Passages

The pink fingers of dawn had barely touched the Alexandria harbour when Youssef appeared at their boat, his weathered face tense with urgency.

"The Vatican agents have sealed off the airport and cruise terminals", he whispered, handing them each a set of clothes and papers. "They've distributed your descriptions to port authorities and border checkpoints. Alexandria has become a trap".

Sarah exchanged a worried glance with James as they changed into the simple garb of Egyptian locals- loose cotton clothing that concealed both their features and the evidence they carried. The documents from Father Mikhail were secured in special waterproof pouches strapped beneath their clothes.

"So how do we get out?" James asked, studying the identity papers Youssef had provided.

"The same way Christians have escaped persecution in this city for two thousand years". Youssef smiled grimly, pointing downwards. "Below the streets".

He led them through a labyrinth of narrow alleys in the old fisherman's quarter, where washing lines created a canopy overhead and the scent of morning bread mingled with sea salt. Twice, they doubled back, using reflective surfaces to spot the dark-suited men searching for them. At one point, they slipped out of a crowded morning market just as three Vatican agents appeared at its entrance.

"Cardinal Romano has deployed his full resources", Youssef muttered as they ducked into a centuries-old Coptic church. Inside, the priest nodded silently and moved aside an ornate prayer stand, revealing worn stone steps descending into darkness.

"The catacombs", Sarah breathed. "I'd read about them but I thought most were sealed or collapsed".

"The official ones, yes", Youssef replied. "These are different- pathways known only

164

to those who've needed to preserve truth through the centuries. They connect to a network that extends all the way to a private airfield outside the city".

As they descended, the air grew thick with history. Youssef turned on an electric lantern, illuminating walls carved with ancient Coptic symbols- many matching those they'd seen in the Monastery's hidden chambers.

"Navigation markers", James explained, recognising a particular sequence. "The same system the Guardians used in London and Cambridge".

"The network reaches farther than you imagine", Youssef said. "When Nicaea's changes began spreading, believers created these escape routes. Alexandria was once the centre of Christian learning- before they altered the message".

They moved deeper into the labyrinth, passing chambers where the light beams from their flashlights revealed hidden alcoves filled with clay pots.

"More evidence?" Sarah asked, pausing to examine one.

"Yes, but we can't stop now". Youssef urged them forward. "Your plane won't wait and the Vatican teams are already searching the known catacombs".

The rumble of footsteps echoed above. They froze, huddling against the ancient stone as dust filtered down from the ceiling.

"They're inside the church", James whispered.

Youssef extinguished their light, plunging them into complete darkness. They waited, barely breathing, as voices and flashlight beams swept the chamber above. A door slammed. Then silence.

"That was too close", Sarah whispered when Youssef finally turned the lantern back on. "How much farther?"

"There", he pointed to a symbol etched into the wall- a dove carrying what looked like a scroll. "The eastern passage. We're halfway there".

The tunnels narrowed as they continued, forcing them to crouch at times. The air grew fresher as they approached what appeared to be a dead end. Youssef pressed a sequence of stones, and a section of wall slid aside with a grinding whisper of ancient mechanisms.

They emerged into an abandoned warehouse at Alexandria's eastern edge. Through a dusty window, Sarah could see the desert stretching toward the horizon.

"The airfield is three kilometres from here", Youssef said, leading them to a battered truck hidden beneath a tarp. "Malcolm's contact will be waiting with your plane".

As the warehouse door slid open, they heard the distinct sound of car engines approaching.

"They've found us", James said, checking the magazine of his weapon.

"No", Youssef replied calmly. "That's your diversion". He pointed to a convoy of identical trucks, each leaving from different warehouses along the street. "All heading to different airfields. The Vatican teams will have to split up to follow them all".

"That's brilliant", Sarah said, understanding dawning. "Malcolm arranged this?"

"The Guardians have been preparing for this moment for centuries", Youssef reminded them as they climbed into the truck. "This is not the first time evidence has needed protection, nor will it be the last".

The truck rumbled to life, joining the convoy briefly before splitting off onto a side road. In the side mirror, Sarah could see black SUVs scrambling to follow the various vehicles, their resources stretched too thin.

An hour later, they approached a small airstrip where another Cessna waited, its engines already running. Malcolm's contact- a young woman with military precision in her movements- hurried them aboard.

"Multiple Vatican teams have been diverted to the main airport and three decoy locations", she reported to James. "You have a clear window of approximately twenty minutes before they realise, they've been tricked".

As their plane taxied for take-off, Sarah looked out the window at the ancient city. After a few minutes, which felt more like hours, their plane finally lifted into the air and the city receded beneath them. Alexandria- where the earliest Christians had preserved the truth, where the great library had once housed knowledge and where a network of believers still fought to protect the evidence of Christianity's transformation- was disappearing from sight. *Will I ever see you again, beautiful city?* Sarah asked herself quietly.

"Jerusalem next", James said, checking his secure phone. "Father Thomas is already there, tracking down the final evidence".

The plane lifted into the morning sky, leaving behind a trail of frustrated Vatican agents and the guardians who had protected them.

The truth had survived Alexandria's dangers. The hunt would continue in the Holy City,

where it had all begun two thousand years
before.

CHAPTER 15: The Flight to Jerusalem

The plane was cruising at 38,000 feet, its engines humming steadily as below the white sands of the desert gradually turned brown. Soon, they would be flying over the Sinai desert. They wouldn't see Mount Sinai- where Moses had ascended the mountain to receive the Ten Commandments, written on tablets engraved by God's finger. That mountain range was too far south of their flight path.

They had struggled to evade the Vatican's agents at the airport but Malcolm had arranged yet another diversion. Fortunately, his distractions had worked.

Sarah looked at the documents spread across the small table between her and James, the cabin's soft lighting giving the ancient parchments an ethereal glow.

"I still can't believe the Vatican's willing to kill to keep this hidden", she said, organising the papers into categories-correspondence, meeting minutes, planning documents. Each piece adding to the puzzle of Christianity's transformation. "What could be so threatening about different versions of the Bible?"

James smiled his infuriating half-smile that made her pulse quicken. Even after all their time together, he still had that effect on her. "How much do you know about the LOGOS Bible?"

"Honestly? Not much. I'd never heard of it until this week".

James leaned back in his seat, but his eyes were intense. "Most haven't. The LOGOS Bible described by first-century Christians is at the very heart of everything we've uncovered. Their LOGOS Bible is Christianity as it was meant to be- before Paul's additions, before Tertius's epistle, before Caiaphas's orchestrations".

Sarah's academic interest was piqued. The way he said "LOGOS Bible"- like it was something sacred and dangerous at the same time- made her lean forward. "Different from our standard sixty-six book version?"

"Very". James's voice took on the tone she recognised from their coffee shop debates- passionate, precise but this time without the artificial scepticism he'd used to maintain his cover. "The LOGOS Bible has forty-nine books total: thirty-nine Old Testament Books but just ten books from the New Testament. By the way, the ancients called this ten-book New Testament- the Apostolic Scriptures".

"That name makes sense. But only ten books?" Sarah's brow furrowed. She'd spent years studying biblical manuscripts, but this was something entirely new. "Which ones?"

James counted them off on his fingers, each name carrying weight. "The Gospels of Matthew and John and the Epistles of James, First and Second Peter, First, Second and Third John and Jude. Revelation is the tenth book".

"But those are all written by---"

"Christ's actual Apostles", James finished. "The men He personally chose to be His Disciples". He pulled out his phone and tapped open his Bible app to Matthew 10.

173

"Here's the list of the twelve He chose. You know them: Simon Peter, Andrew, James and John the sons of Zebedee, Philip, Bartholomew, Thomas, Matthew the tax collector, James- son of Alphaeus, Thaddaeus- who also wrote under the name Jude, Simon the Zealot and Judas Iscariot".

Sarah's mind was already racing with the implications of this information. "So, the LOGOS Bible's New Testament only includes books written by the men who are on this list? The ones who were actually with Jesus?"

"Exactly". James's eyes lit up with scholarly passion. "Remember John 17:6-8? Jesus said the Father gave these men to Him and that *their very words would come from God Himself.* That's why the Guardians have protected this truth for so long. These ten books represent Christ's message in its purest form- before Paul's additions changed everything".

Sarah frowned, her expertise in biblical manuscripts raising immediate questions.

"But what about the gospels of Mark and Luke? Or the other epistles?"

"That's where it gets interesting". James lowered his voice, even though they were alone on the plane. The intimacy of the moment made her heart race. "Biblical scholars have tied themselves up in knots trying to explain why the Gospels of Matthew, Mark and Luke are so similar. They've invented terms like 'Q Source' and 'Marcan Priority' to try and explain it".

"I know the theories", Sarah said, remembering countless academic debates. "They suggest Mark was written first and later Matthew and Luke copied from Mark and this hypothetical 'Q' source".

"But what if they've got it backwards?" James leaned forward, his enthusiasm contagious. "What if Matthew wrote first, as an actual eyewitness and Mark and Luke-who were Paul's associates- copied elements of *his* apostolic account to fit their new version of Christianity?"

Sarah sat back, her thoughts swirling. "So, the similarities..."

175

"Are because later writers built on the apostolic accounts and then added their own interpretations".

"James- this puts a whole new perspective on how Luke begins his gospel account. Funny, I had always wondered about that passage". Sarah sat quietly, trying to remember the exact words of Luke's first chapter. "Can you pull up what he said on your phone?"

James tapped his phone to open his Bible app again and began reading,

> 'Forasmuch as many have taken in hand to set forth in order a declaration of those things which are most surely believed among us, Even as they delivered them unto us, which from the beginning were eyewitnesses, and ministers of the word; It seemed good to me also, having had perfect understanding of all things from the very first, to write unto thee in order, most excellent Theophilus, That thou mightiest

know the certainty of those things,
wherein thou hast been instructed.'

Both sat quietly for a few minutes. The
words from the first four verses of Luke's
gospel floated in the air.

"That's just like a confession", Sarah finally
exclaimed. "He's actually admitting that he
is one of many who copied from the
Apostles- 'which from the beginning were
eyewitnesses'".

"Exactly".

"But James, even if Luke copied from the
Apostles, maybe Mark and Luke acted
independently. Maybe they had nothing to
do with Caiaphas and Paul's manipulations.
Maybe they didn't even know Paul or each
other".

Sarah leaned back in her seat and closed her
eyes. There was something she remembered
reading in one of Paul's letters about this but
she couldn't remember exactly what it was.
"But I seem to remember something in one
of Paul's epistles…" her voice trailed off.

"You're right, Sarah. Actually, Paul confirms not once but on two occasions that the three of them worked together- in 2 Timothy 4:11 and in Philemon 1:24. Paul called Mark and Luke his fellow labourers! Today, we would call them his accomplices".

"So, the evidence was there for biblical scholars, if they had wanted to see it..." Sarah added softly.

James tapped through more documents on his phone. "And it goes deeper than just which books belong in scripture. The LOGOS Bible presents a radically different understanding of core Christian concepts".

"Like what?"

"Well, for example, take the nature of God", James answered. "The LOGOS Bible maintains a clear distinction- one eternal God, the Father, with Jesus as His divine but created Son. No Trinity doctrine".

"That would certainly shake up two thousand years of Christian theology", Sarah murmured, understanding the implications.

"Exactly. Do you remember why Christ said He would make Peter the rock upon which He would build His church? Think back to Matthew 16 16. Peter never called Christ- 'God'. He understood that Christ was the '*Son* of the living God'. But the Trinity doctrine has tried to change our understanding of this".

James paused. *Maybe Sarah has heard enough*, he thought. *But if anything happened to him, Sarah has to be able to defend the LOGOS Bible.* He decided to keep going.

"But the really revolutionary part of the LOGOS Bible is what it teaches us about salvation and judgment". James selected one of the Bermondsey documents. "The LOGOS Bible teaches that salvation requires both faith *and* works, with final judgment based on our works- just as Jesus said it would in Matthew 16:27, Matthew 25:31-46 and Revelation 20:12-15".

Sarah's mind was already connecting dots. "So, when Caiaphas, Paul and Tertius introduced the concept of salvation by faith alone..."

James nodded. "They fundamentally altered Christ's message of personal accountability. They created a Christianity that was more palatable to power structures. Their version doesn't require us to *focus on doing the right things*- like fighting against injustice or fighting for social justice".

"What about church structure?" Sarah asked, fully engaged now.

"The LOGOS Bible presents the ecclesia as a governing legislative body, not a hierarchy of church officials. And the Great Commission is really about teaching truth, not converting people to a particular belief system". James checked his watch. "We've got another 45 minutes together before we get to the Ben Gurion Airport. Want me to walk you through how the LOGOS Bible addresses end times prophecies? It's fascinating stuff".

Sarah smiled, reaching for her notebook again. The way he said 'together' made her stomach flutter. "Tell me everything".

James spent the next ten minutes explaining how the LOGOS Bible interpreted apocalyptic prophecies and showed how the addition of non-apostolic books had clouded the understanding of end times events.

Sarah realised that James was a man of very deep faith. *How had he kept this side of himself so well hidden*, she wondered to herself, during a lull in their conversation.

Sarah lifted her head from her note taking to look at him directly. "James", she asked. "I would like to know more. Are you okay to keep going?"

"Of course", he answered with a warm smile on his face. "I'm happy this interests you so much, Sarah. It's very important to me".

"Tell me about forgiveness, James. Help me to understand why Jesus focused on it so much".

"That's a very perceptive question. Most people don't realise that Christ's message of forgiveness is similar to the Old Testament's advice regarding vengeance. Remember the- 'vengeance is mine sayeth the LORD' statement? The real message is not actually about forgiveness or vengeance! It's about whether you truly believe in a God who can and will fight for justice on your behalf- so *you* don't have to. If you truly believe, then you will be able to let go and let God".

"Let go and let God", Sarah repeated quietly. "So, when I truly forgive someone, what the LOGOS Bible teaches is- 'I believe God will give me the justice I deserve someday?'" Sarah leaned back into her seat. "That's deep…"

"Sarah, everything in the LOGOS Bible- from Genesis to Revelation- boils down to one question and one answer. 'Do you believe in God?' is the question and 'Yes, I believe' is the answer".

"James- we're arriving soon. Just give me a list of the other main differences between the LOGOS Bible and the 66-book version. Wow- who knew!"

"Sure, Sarah. No problem. First, there's how we are supposed to live our lives in *active faith*. That's what Matthew 6:33 means- seeking first the kingdom of God. God wants to see charity, not piety. Another one is keeping the proper Sabbath- Friday sundown to Saturday sundown. Sunday is not God's Sabbath! Do you know, Sarah, that most people don't realise that the Ten Commandments were given in order of importance? Think about it. And because of that- God is sending us an important message when the 'Honour My Sabbath' commandment comes before the 'Thou shalt not kill' commandment! God *really* cares which day of the week we choose to worship Him. Our choice of Sabbath day indicates our belief in His creation account. Remember, a *Saturday* Sabbath is only important because it is the day that God said to rest- after He finished creating everything. But if you don't actually believe that God created the heavens and the earth and everything in them, then the choice to worship on a Saturday or Sunday won't really make a difference to you".

James continued. "Ok, another difference is 'speaking in tongues'. Mark and Paul say it is a sign of true faith". He stopped and rolled his eyes in contempt at this idea before continuing. "But Christ never did it. He never spoke in tongues. He never talked about it. He never taught it. You get the picture.

James looked directly at Sarah. "Do you believe me now when I said there were differences between the two messages? Do you want me to keep going?"

"Keep going".

"Another difference is interfaith dialogue and respect. The LOGOS Bible teaches us that the believers of the various Abrahamic faiths pray to the *same* God- Jehovah, YHWH, Allah. We are all the people of God. Gender equality is another difference. Christ saw men and women as equals. He never told women to be quiet or prohibited them from any roles in the Church or in their communities. Even in the Old Testament, women ruled as queens, judges and prophets".

"And look at how many years we've wasted in human history fighting for equal rights, when this is what was ordained for everyone all along!" Sarah exclaimed.

James continued. "The same thing with the LGBTQ community. Not one time, Sarah, in any of the apostolic writings did Christ ever admonish or ostracise this community".

James paused. "Are you getting all of this?"

"Yes, I am", she answered.

"Do you know", James started again. "I love watching American football. One of the best Superbowl TV commercials I ever saw was by the 'He Gets Us' organisation. It was excellent. Spot on target. I think it was first released about three years ago. 'Love your neighbour' was the message. Have you ever seen their ads?"

"I have. That one touched me too. Jesus doesn't want us splicing and dicing people. Who's eligible, who's not eligible. Our duty is to love…"

"Exactly. Simple message. But so hard for people to do". After a period of thoughtful silence, James said, "Sarah- I could keep going on and on. There are other theological differences, of course, but the ones I've been explaining to you are some of the main ones.

You can see that these differences govern our relationship with God and with one another. Imagine what our world might have been like if most Christians had been taught Christ's real message…"

"True", Sarah responded. "But now I finally understand why some atheists, agnostics and even former Christians have rejected Christianity. What they saw as doctrinal contradictions and inconsistencies were actually due to the effects of Caiaphas's opposing messages planted on purpose. Wow! I need to think about this for a little while".

Later, as Sarah finished reading her notes, patterns began emerging- patterns that went beyond just the theological implications.

"James", she said suddenly. He was looking at the Alexandria documents.

"How many authors wrote the Apostolic Scriptures?"

"Five", he replied. "Why?"

"And there are ten books in the Apostolic Scriptures?" Her fingers moved across her notebook as she double-checked her notes. "And the LOGOS Bible has forty-nine books in total..."

James's eyes lit up, understanding where she was going. "You've spotted the numerical patterns".

"In biblical numerology, five represents God's grace, doesn't it? And ten represents divine order". Sarah's voice grew excited as the pieces fell into place. "Seven represents spiritual perfection and forty-nine is seven times seven..."

"Representing extraordinary spiritual perfection", James finished, his voice soft in approval. "While six represents man and sixty-six..."

"The number of books in the traditional Bible". Sarah sat back, stunned. "Even the numbers tell a story, don't they? Five apostolic authors, ten apostolic books, forty-nine total books in the LOGOS Bible- all numbers representing divine grace, order and perfection".

"While six is the number of man, sixty-six is the number of books in the Bible that Caiaphas and Paul created and six hundred and sixty-six is the number of the anti-christ. All the sixes..." James's voice trailed off meaningfully.

"The truth was hidden in plain sight all along", Sarah whispered. "Even in the numbers themselves".

They sat in silence for a moment, the weight of what they'd discussed settling between them. Sarah found herself wondering how many others throughout history had seen these patterns, had tried to expose what they'd found, only to be silenced.

The evidence they'd gathered on their travels and whatever else awaited them in Jerusalem, would give them a chance to show the world what Christianity was meant to be. But only if they lived long enough to share it.

James noticed her distraction. "Having second thoughts?"

She thought of the Yair Letter that had started everything, of the truth hidden in plain sight for two thousand years. Of the way James looked at her now, like she was part of something greater than herself. "No. People deserve to know what really happened. What Christianity was supposed to be".

James looked deeply into her eyes. "Even if it changes everything?"

Sarah met his eyes, feeling the chemistry between them crackling like electricity. "Especially if it changes everything".

The plane flew on through the morning sun, carrying them toward answers that had been buried in the Tomb of Joseph of Arimathaea since the first century. And somewhere below, multiple Vatican agents were already converging on their destination.

The race to expose the truth was about to enter its final phase. Whatever challenges lay ahead. Sarah knew one thing for certain- she and James would face them together.

The truth about Christianity's transformation couldn't stay hidden forever. And maybe, just maybe, something else was transforming too- something between a brilliant researcher and the Guardian who'd been waiting for her to discover the truth.

CHAPTER 16: The Arimathaean Chamber

The flight time to Jerusalem had passed quickly with all their discussions.

The ancient city spread beneath them as their plane descended, golden in the midday light. But there was no time to admire the view.

As they waited for their car, Sarah studied her tablet while James monitored the Vatican communications that Malcolm had intercepted.

"Malcolm says- 'Multiple teams converging on Jerusalem. They know we have the Alexandria Letters'".

"At least we know why they're so desperate to stop this". Sarah enlarged a particular passage on her tablet. "You know Caiaphas laid out exactly how they would dismantle Christ's message of social justice- step by step, generation by generation".

"Until people forgot there was ever a different version of Christianity". James

191

moved to sit beside her. "Where did Father Thomas say to meet him?"

"He just sent coordinates". Sarah showed him the message. "But I recognise the location- it's near the Temple Mount".

Finally, their Guardian vehicle arrived. They jumped in and started on a circuitous route to shake off any followers.

"Something's been bothering me", Sarah said as James was navigating the narrow streets. "Caiaphas's journal explains why they changed Christianity but Father Thomas' message mentioned finding 'what they feared most.' What if there's more?"

"There is". The voice came from the back seat, making them both jump. Father Thomas sat up from where he'd been hiding under a blanket.

"You could have warned us", James said but he was smiling.

"Couldn't risk the message being intercepted". The elderly scholar looked exhausted but his eyes were bright. "What I found in Egypt- it's not just evidence of their conspiracy. It's proof that others tried to expose the truth before".

He pulled a small package from his coat. Inside was a collection of ancient parchments, carefully preserved.

"These were hidden in that sealed chamber. Letters from bishops who opposed what happened at Nicaea. They documented everything- how the Council was manipulated, how Paul's writings were added to scripture and all the doctrinal changes"

"We found similar evidence in Alexandria", Sarah told him.

"But did you find this?" Father Thomas held up a particular document. "It's a letter from the Coptic Pope of that era. He wrote it the night before the crucial votes at Nicaea".

Sarah accepted the delicate parchment, reading: "'Tomorrow they will cement their changes into doctrine. But they forget- truth cannot be hidden forever. We have preserved the evidence of their deception and, more importantly, we have preserved copies of the original apostolic testimonies. The true message of Christ, the LOGOS Bible, will survive. And when the time is right, when the world most needs this message of justice and accountability, it will be released'".

"The LOGOS Bible", James said quietly. "Forty-nine books containing the pure message".

"Which is why we need to get to our next location". Father Thomas checked his watch. "The Vatican teams are searching the wrong places. They think we're after more evidence of the conspiracy. But there's something far more important hidden here in Jerusalem".

"What?" James and Sarah exclaimed in unison.

"Proof that the LOGOS Bible was the original compilation. Proof that all the added books- Paul's letters, Mark, Luke, Hebrews- were exactly that: additions designed to change Christ's message".

A vehicle appeared in their mirror- a black SUV with tinted windows. *Just like London*, Sarah thought.

194

"Time to move", James said. "Where exactly are we going?"

"The Tomb of Joseph of Arimathaea", Father Thomas answered.

Sarah turned to stare at him. "I thought that was just a legend. No one knows where it really is".

"The Guardians in Jerusalem do". Father Thomas smiled. "Remember what the Yair Letter said- secure locations were used to protect the original apostolic testimonies and the evidence of the conspiracy. Maybe Joseph of Arimathaea didn't just provide his tomb for Christ's burial. Maybe he also provided a secure location for preserving evidence of the truth. Think about it- who would look for hidden documents in a tomb everyone believes is lost?"

The SUV was getting closer. James took a sharp turn down a narrow alley, barely wide enough for their car.

"They told me the entrance is beneath the Old City", Father Thomas continued. "But we'll have to time this perfectly. Too many people are searching for us, too many eyes are watching".

"Why didn't you tell us about this before?" Sarah asked.

"Because I needed to confirm something first. Those records about Nicaea- they're not just evidence of a conspiracy. They're the irrefutable proof that Caiaphas and Paul did exactly what Jesus warned about in His Matthew 13 prophecy".

"The wheat and tares", Sarah whispered. "Growing together until the harvest".

"Exactly. They planted their altered version of Christianity right alongside the truth..."

A bullet shattered their back window.

"Save the theology for later", James said, accelerating through the ancient streets. "Where exactly is this entrance?"

Father Thomas directed them through a maze of alleys, finally stopping beside what looked like an abandoned storage room built into the city wall. Once inside the storage room, he quickly moved aside some crates, revealing an ancient stone shaft descending into darkness.

"This is supposed to be the original entrance to Joseph's tomb complex", he explained as they climbed down. "And the place where he hid something far more valuable than gold- proof that the LOGOS Bible represents Christianity as it was meant to be".

In the distance, they could hear men shouting. The voices sounded anxious. But Sarah hardly noticed. Her attention was fixed on the chamber ahead, where ancient oil lamps, waiting to be lit, still hung on walls covered in first-century writing.

"Oh my gosh", she whispered. "It must all be here. Everything we need to prove the truth must be here".

As they got closer to the walls of the chamber, Sarah's torch light illuminated an ancient inscription carved above the entrance. She paused, studying the faded characters.

"There's something written here", she said, her fingers tracing the worn symbols.

Father Thomas moved closer, squinting in the dim light. "Can you make it out?"

Sarah nodded slowly, her expertise in ancient languages allowing her to decipher what others might miss. "It's actually in Hebrew and not Aramaic, surprisingly...five words: 'Limmud Otsar Galah Orach Shemaya'".

"What does it mean?" James asked.

"In English it means- 'Learn the treasures of the LORD which reveal the path to heaven'", Sarah translated, her voice hushed with reverence. "I think it's a declaration of purpose for this chamber- that it houses the authentic teachings".

James suddenly straightened, his eyes widening. "Wait- say those Hebrew words again".

"Limmud... Otsar... Galah... Orach... Shemaya". Sarah repeated, then gasped as understanding dawned. "L-O-G-O-S. The first letters spell LOGOS!"

"Exactly", James said, excitement building in his voice. "But not the Greek word 'Logos' meaning 'the Word' or 'God's reason', as later Greek-speaking Christians would assume. This is a Hebrew acronym-hidden in plain sight for centuries".

Father Thomas's eyes lit with understanding. "So that explains why they called a collection of Hebrew and Aramaic writings-the 'LOGOS Bible'. It wasn't a Greek name at all but a first-century Hebrew code, used by those who knew the truth. Just like the fish symbol for Christianity- 'IChThYS'. True believers could stay safely hidden in plain sight".

"A brilliant safeguard", James replied. "Later generations of Greek-speaking believers naturally assumed the name referred to the Greek philosophical concept of 'Logos' because of how they interpreted the Greek version of John's Gospel opening. But all along, it was actually this Hebrew acronym pointing to the authentic teachings".

Sarah shook her head in amazement. "Two thousand years of misinterpretation... even the name itself was part of the mystery".

"And another layer of evidence showing which writings were authentic", James added. "The original preservers marked them with this acronym, only for it to be misunderstood as the Greek term".

As they stepped through the entrance, the weight of this revelation added new significance to what they were hoping to discover inside.

CHAPTER 17: The CHI-RO Cross

The tomb chamber was larger than Sarah expected, its walls covered in detailed Aramaic text. The light from their flashlights cast shadows as Father Thomas led them deeper into the complex.

"Joseph of Arimathaea didn't just hide documents here", he explained. "He created a testimony in stone- a record of how Christianity was meant to be and how they began changing it. The walls themselves tell the story".

Sarah moved closer, translating: "'From the beginning, we knew what they planned. Even as the Apostles wrote their testimonies, others were preparing to change their message. But we were ready. Those of us who believed, who recognised Jesus as Messiah while serving in the Temple, began preserving evidence of the truth...'"

Above them, footsteps echoed through the Old City streets. The Vatican agents were getting closer.

201

"Here." James's torch illuminated a particular section of text. "This shows exactly how they did it. Step by step".

Sarah read aloud: "'First came Paul's letters, introducing concepts the Apostles never taught. Then Mark's account, then Luke's account, all subtly shifting focus from the Father to Christ. They created new doctrines- making Christ equal to God and they replaced the message of active justice with one of passive faith...'"

"But that's not the most important part", Father Thomas said. He directed their attention to a sealed niche in the wall. "This is what I discovered references to while I was in Egypt- it's the reason I had to be certain before bringing you here".

The niche contained a clay jar, similar to those that had preserved the Dead Sea Scrolls. Inside was a collection of parchments that made Sarah's hands tremble as she read them.

"These are letters from the original apostolic communities", she breathed. "Writing to each other about what was happening, recording how they preserved Christ's true message. Look- actual correspondence between the churches about which books belonged in scripture and which didn't".

"Keep reading", Father Thomas urged.

"'We have hidden copies of the authentic scriptures- the testimony of the Apostles and the Books of old. Forty-nine books that contain the pure message, before their additions. Let those who find this know: what you have called the Bible has been changed. But the truth survives in what later generations will call the LOGOS Bible...'".

A noise from the entrance shaft made them all freeze.

"Multiple teams converging", James reported, checking his phone. "We're running out of time".

"Then let me show you another reason why I brought you here". Father Thomas moved to the chamber's far wall, pressing a series of ancient stones. A section of wall slid aside, revealing another room. "Yet another reason they're so desperate to stop us".

The hidden chamber took Sarah's breath away. Floor-to-ceiling shelves held clay jars, each one numbered and sealed with symbols she recognised from their discoveries in Egypt and Alexandria.

"The complete evidence", Father Thomas said quietly. "Records from every major Christian centre, documenting how the changes spread. Letters between churches trying to resist. Warnings about what was being lost. But more importantly...", he moved to a particular shelf, removing two jars carefully. "Proof that others throughout history discovered this truth and tried to expose it".

Sarah opened the first jar, finding more letters inside. "*These are from different centuries*! You mean- these are from people who found evidence of the conspiracy and tried to reveal it?"

"Each time someone got close to exposing the truth, they were stopped. If their evidence was found, it was destroyed, their voices silenced. But some managed to have their testimonies preserved here, adding to Joseph's original collection".

"And now it's our turn", James said. "But this time we have something they didn't".

"The ability to share the truth instantly, globally". Sarah understood. "No wonder they're so worried".

The first sounds of someone descending the entrance shaft echoed through the tomb.

"Time to go", James said. "Tell me there's another way out".

"Through here". Father Thomas was already moving deeper into the chamber. "The same tunnels the early believers used to preserve the evidence. They'll take us to---"

The bullet caught him in the shoulder, spinning him against the ancient shelves. More shots followed as Vatican agents began swarming into the chamber.

"The jars!" Sarah grabbed as many as she could, shoving them into her backpack while James returned fire, covering them.

"You won't be able to hide those documents forever!" Cardinal Romano's voice echoed through the tomb. "You don't have to do this!"

"We no longer have a choice!" Sarah called back. "You've been protecting those who changed Christ's message. You're helping to make people forget what Christianity was supposed to be!"

They retreated into the tunnel system, James half-carrying Father Thomas. Behind them, more voices joined the Cardinal's. The Vatican teams were following them but they didn't know which of the tunnels they had disappeared into.

"James!" she whispered as she grabbed his arm, pointing to a particular series of markings on the wall. "We have to check this out. These are Roman military symbols-used by Roman intelligence officers".

Their tunnel suddenly opened into a vast chamber; its high ceiling lost in darkness. Ancient oil lamps still sat in wall niches, their bronze surfaces green with age. But it was the chamber's contents that made them all stop short.

"Oh my gosh", Sarah gasped. "It's an archive filled with Roman intelligence documents".

Row upon row of sealed clay jars lined stone shelves, each bearing imperial seals and military coding. A stone table dominated the centre, its surface covered in what looked like battle maps- but the targets weren't military installations.

"They're early Christian communities", James said, studying the maps. "Every major centre of apostolic teaching. Look at the dates- all before Nicaea".

Sarah moved to examine the jars. "These are field reports. Roman agents infiltrating Christian groups, identifying leaders, tracking the spread of..." She paused, translating. "The 'dangerous doctrine'".

"Here, you must take these!" Father Thomas tried to pull a bundle of scrolls from a particular jar. "These are sealed with the Chi-Rho cross".

"We have to get this evidence out", Sarah said. "Let the world see what they did- and why".

Father Thomas pressed a jar into her hands, his voice weak but urgent. "This one. Make sure this one survives. It proves everything- how they changed it, why they changed it and most importantly...on whose orders the changes were made".

They came out of the chamber and kept running down the tunnel. James was still helping Father Thomas to move. The tunnel forked ahead of them. James checked his phone. "We'll go right. The Guardian team is standing by at the Damascus Gate. If we get this evidence out, then there's no stopping the truth from spreading".

Sarah held the precious jar close, thinking of all those throughout history who had tried to expose this truth. This time would be different. This time, the world would know.

"Ready?" James asked.

She nodded. They had the evidence. They had the truth. Now they just had to survive long enough to share it with the world.

CHAPTER 18: The Damascus Gate

The Damascus Gate loomed ahead as they emerged from the tunnel system. Sarah clutched the jars containing their precious evidence while James supported Father Thomas, whose shoulder was still bleeding.

A Guardian met them at the gate with medical support and a secure vehicle. As they sped through Jerusalem's ancient streets, Sarah carefully examined the first jar's contents.

"These aren't just more conspiracy documents", she said, her voice tight with excitement. "They're letters from the Alexandrian church- actual proof that the forty-nine-book compilation was the true word".

Father Thomas winced as a medic tried to clean his wound in the speeding car. "Read the letter dated just before Nicaea".

Sarah found it, translating: "'We see what is coming. At Nicaea, they will make their changes official- adding Paul's writings to scripture, establishing new doctrines that dilute Christ's message. But we have preserved the truth. The pure compilation, the LOGOS Bible, will survive'".

Sarah continued reading. "'In Alexandria, we maintain copies of the original manuscripts. Forty-nine books containing the complete message of justice and accountability. Let future generations know- what the Council will establish is not what the Apostles taught. The changes began with Paul but, at Nicaea, they will complete their transformation of Christianity'".

James received an update on his phone. 'Vatican teams have split up. Some following us, others heading to the airport'.

"They think we're trying to leave the country", Father Thomas said. "But they don't know about the Guardian safe house facility here in Jerusalem".

Their vehicle turned down a series of increasingly narrow streets before entering what appeared to be an abandoned warehouse. Inside, modern technology mixed with ancient stone architecture.

212

"This is the perfect place to examine what we've found", Father Thomas explained as Guardian medical staff helped him to a chair.

They cut through his outer clothing to expose his bare left shoulder. After a thorough cleaning with an antiseptic solution, the medics examined his left shoulder in detail. Fortunately, it was just a flesh wound. No hospital visit required. Within ten minutes, Father Thomas's shoulder had been bandaged and his arm was placed in a sling for support.

The medics tidied their makeshift work area and left.

Sarah carefully laid out their evidence on a scanning table. The documents were even more revealing than she'd hoped.

"Look at this- detailed records of how the early church really operated, before Paul's influence. Their focus on social justice, on personal accountability, on building God's kingdom through action, not just faith..."

"And this", James pointed to a particular passage. "Instructions for preserving evidence of the changes: 'Hide copies in multiple locations. Let each generation add their testimony of how Christianity was altered. One day, when humanity most needs Christ's true message, all of this will be found'".

Sarah's hands trembled as she read the next letter: "'We see the changes happening already. Paul's writings are spreading and becoming more popular, changing the focus from justice to passive faith. His doctrines- making Christ equal to God, shifting the emphasis from accountability to grace alone. With each generation, fewer remember what Christianity was meant to be...'".

Father Thomas joined them at the table, his shoulder pain now easing after treatment. "But the most important evidence is still in that jar that you're holding".

Sarah opened the jar carefully. Inside was a collection of papers that looked different from the others- more official, more formal.

"These are original documents from Nicaea itself", she breathed. "Meeting minutes that were never meant to survive. Lists of bishops who opposed the changes but were silenced...".

"Keep going", Father Thomas urged. "Get to the final pages".

Sarah's eyes widened as she read: "'Let it be recorded- we, the undersigned bishops, protest these changes to Christ's message. We reject the elevation of Paul's writings to scripture. We reject the doctrine of the Trinity. We reject the emphasis on faith without works. These changes serve only to protect power, to prevent the social transformation that Christ's true message would bring...'".

"Complete with their signatures", James noted. "Actual proof of opposition at Nicaea".

"Opposition that was erased from official church history", Father Thomas added. "Until now".

Sarah laid out the final documents. "Instructions for future generations. Explaining how to recognise the true message when it re-emerges: 'Look for these signs- an emphasis on social justice, on personal accountability, on a distinction between God and Christ. This was Christianity before they changed it. This is what the LOGOS Bible preserves...'".

A security alert flashed on the facility's screens. Vatican teams had found them.

Sarah had one more jar to open- the jar with the Roman military symbols. "Oh my gosh", Sarah whispered to herself. She couldn't believe her eyes. Here was rock-solid proof that Christianity's transformation had been orchestrated at the highest levels of Roman power. She turned to speak to James, who was trying to find an escape route out. "James- the world has to see this. These scrolls bear Constantine's wax seal with his Chi-Rho cross".

Sarah's hands trembled as she unrolled the first document. "This one's called- 'Strategic Assessment'", she translated. "'The Christian sect presents unique opportunities and dangers. Their message of universal justice and divine equality threatens the established order. *However, properly modified, their beliefs could serve imperial interests...*".

The next document made her gasp. "James, this is it- the actual orders. From Constantine himself to his intelligence chief: 'The solution presents itself. We shall convene a council, gather their bishops, create a unified doctrine. Caiaphas's plan, implemented through Saul, provided an excellent foundation. Now, we shall institutionalise these changes. Create a religion that preaches submission to authority while promising rewards in the next life. On my direct orders- change the rest day from Saturday to Sunday. Those who comply are loyal to my version of Christianity. Those who refuse must be put to death- I am not interested in their loyalty to God's Commandments'".

She kept reading, her voice tight with tension: "'The dangerous elements must be permanently suppressed- their teaching of equality between men and women, their

217

acceptance of all peoples, their insistence on active faith over mere belief. Create new doctrines. Make Christ equal to God, thereby diluting the Father's authority. Establish complex church hierarchies. Above all, eliminate their message of personal accountability and social justice'".

Sarah grabbed another scroll: "'Our Nicaea plan proceeds perfectly. Those who might oppose us have been delayed or eliminated. The doctrine of the Trinity will shift focus from their God's demands for justice. Salvation through faith alone will make them passive and ineffective. Within a generation, no one will remember Christ's original message of transformation...'".

"Political manipulation from the very beginning", James said softly. "The Romans saw the threat in Christ's original message".

Sarah continued reading: "'We cannot allow this message of universal justice to spread. Create new doctrines'".

The elderly scholar was pale but his eyes burned with intensity. "And this is why it still matters today".

Sarah carefully laid out their evidence on a scanning table. Each document revealed a deeper layer of the conspiracy- not just theological changes but deliberate political manipulation of spiritual truths.

The three of them just looked at each other. Their thoughts almost spinning out of control.

If first-century power structures had fought to silence these truths, what would present-day power structures do? There was so much more at stake now.

Would they get out of this together and alive? They did not know.

All the security alerts of the facility were flashing now. Were they trapped? Had the Vatican agents had finally cornered them?

CHAPTER 19: Sheep

"It's time to go", James barked the command as he reached for his weapon.

"No". Father Thomas's voice was firm. "It's time for answers. It's time for the truth".

Just then, the door opened. Cardinal Romano entered first, his silver hair gleaming in the facility's lights. He looked older somehow, tired in a way that went beyond physical exhaustion. He was followed by Luca.

"You don't understand what we've been trying to do", he said to them without preamble.

"We understand exactly what we've uncovered", Sarah replied angrily. "How Christianity was changed. How Paul and Caiaphas deliberately altered Christ's message. How the Council of Nicaea made those changes official. And now we know why- it was all about religious control and political control".

"And you think exposing all of this will make everything better?" he asked. "That returning us to the LOGOS Bible will solve the world's problems?"

"I don't know", Sarah's voice was firm. "But we believe returning to Christ's true message will give people what they need to solve the world's problems *for themselves*. And that's what Caiaphas feared, isn't it? Not just changes to religious authority but to society itself?"

"You found Caiaphas's orders from Senator Silvanus and Constantine's instructions to his intelligence officers". The Cardinal was silent for a long moment. "You know why they did it".

"Because Christ's real message wasn't just about personal salvation", James said. "It was about transforming the world through social justice and personal accountability. It was about people taking responsibility for building God's kingdom right here on earth. Christ's real message was about empowerment- ordinary people believing they could be a part of accomplishing extraordinary things".

"Do you know how many power structures that would threaten?" the Cardinal demanded. "How many systems of control would be challenged if people actually believed they would be held personally accountable by Jesus for not fighting injustice in the world?"

"That's exactly why this information needs to be released", Sarah said quietly. "Look around, Cardinal. Look at what the world has become. People are hungry for real transformation, not just cold porridge religious platitudes. They're ready for the truth".

"And the chaos it will cause? The institutions it will threaten?" he responded.

"Sometimes things need to be threatened", Father Thomas spoke from his chair. "Sometimes transformation requires disruption. You know that's true, David".

The Cardinal was startled at the use of his first name. "You were one of us once,

223

Thomas. You understood why these things
must be controlled...".

"I understood fear", Father Thomas
corrected. "Fear of change, of losing power,
of facing real accountability. But that's not
what Christianity was meant to be".

"Fear of losing power?" the Cardinal said
angrily as he glared at Father Thomas. "I am
surprised to hear that from you- of all
people". He fell silent for a moment to
regain his composure.

The Cardinal turned to face Sarah. "You
think we didn't know what had happened?"
his voice was soft. "You think we've been
trying to destroy the evidence? Sarah, we've
known where these documents were hidden
for centuries. If we had wanted to eliminate
them, we could have done so at any time.
Even now, as we have been chasing you
around the world for the past few days.
Have we destroyed any of the locations that
the three of you discovered were hiding
evidence?"

Sarah stared at him and then looked at James and Father Thomas with a bewildered expression on her face.

"No", she grudgingly admitted. "You haven't destroyed anything".

"The Vatican's role in this...it's more complicated than you can ever imagine". He moved to examine the ancient scrolls on the table in the centre of the room. "We've always known what happened at Nicaea. Known how they changed Christ's message. But we also knew the world wasn't ready for the truth".

"Until now?" Sarah challenged.

"Look around you, Dr. Chen. Look at our world. There are wars and famines. We are on the brink of a global trade war and possibly a world recession. The world is in chaos. Inequality is growing. Social justice movements are being suppressed. Authoritarians are rising. The start of a third world war looks imminent. The powerful are becoming more powerful while the masses are told to wait for heavenly rewards". His finger slowly traced the Chi-Rho cross symbol on the waxed seals of the ancient scrolls.

"And the Vatican?" James's hand on his weapon remained ready, despite the Cardinal's apparent openness. "Where do you stand?"

"Luca", the Cardinal commanded. "Give them the box. Put it on the table for them to open and read for themselves".

Luca stepped forward. In his hands he carried a small iron box bearing Constantine's seal. He placed it on the table in the centre of the room.

Sarah started to move towards the table but James held her back, still wary.

"It's alright". Father Thomas's eyes were clear. "I trust David".

"What you are about to read- this is the real reason Rome had to change Christ's message", Cardinal Romano reminded them.

The box's ancient lock yielded to Sarah's careful touch. Inside lay a single scroll with Constantine's imperial seal unbroken.

"That is an 'Imperial Order'", the Cardinal explained, "from Constantine to his Chief Intelligence Officer. It was intercepted it. Do you remember the Centurion who asked Jesus to heal his servant? The one who had such faith that it amazed Jesus? Matthew included his story in his Gospel".

The three nodded. Everyone knew that story.

The Cardinal continued. "Well, it was one of his descendants who helped us. Many have helped us because of the miracles that Jesus had performed for them, for their family members and for others.

That Centurion's descendant was present when this order was being written. He was asked to deliver it to the Chief Intelligence Officer. He delivered it to us instead and told us what it contained". Cardinal Romano fell silent for a moment. "He was crucified for that act of disobedience. Actually, he was one of the last persons to be crucified before the practise was abolished in the Roman empire".

The Cardinal continued. "This order from Constantine was written after his top military officials had finished evaluating Christ's message. This order explains why Christ's message had to be changed. Not just for religious reasons but for the *very survival of Rome's imperial power"*.

Sarah opened the scroll with trembling hands and broke the seal. As she translated, her voice grew tight with understanding:

"'The danger lies not just in their beliefs about God but in their insistence that divine justice requires human action. They teach that all people- regardless of gender, status or origin- have equal worth and equal responsibility. That true faith requires working for justice in this world and not just waiting for it in the next. Most dangerous of all, they insist that every person will be held personally accountable for their contribution in building God's kingdom on earth.'"

"Keep reading", Father Thomas urged.

"'If Christ's message continues to spread unchanged, *no human system of control can survive*. No hierarchy can stand. No power structure can maintain dominance over people who believe they are divinely empowered and personally accountable for fighting injustice. This Christianity must be modified *or the empire itself will fall.*"'

James took his hand off his weapon. "And nothing's changed. Modern powers still can't allow that message to spread".

"Exactly", the Cardinal's voice was grim. "Why do you think every social justice movement gets branded as dangerous? Why are hierarchies so desperate to maintain control? Why does the modern prosperity gospel keep people focused on personal wealth rather than on social change?"

No one spoke for a few minutes.

"Constantine's plan worked perfectly", Father Thomas said. "Christianity was transformed from a religion of active justice to one of passive faith. From a call to transform the world to a promise of rewards after death. From a message of universal human worth to one of hierarchical authority".

Sarah read the scroll's final lines: "'Implement these changes gradually.

Promote the writings that emphasise faith over works. Create complex doctrines to occupy their minds. Within a few generations, none will remember that Christianity was meant to be a force for real transformation. None will recall that Christ's message wasn't just about personal salvation- it was about creating divine justice on earth'".

"Now you understand", the Cardinal gestured to their evidence, "why this truth matters. Why it threatens power structures as much today as it did then". He stopped speaking and sank into a chair.

He looked at each of them in turn. "And there's more".

"More?" exclaimed Sarah.

"There is something the three of you also need to understand about the Vatican's motives".

He began to speak again. "How many times does Christ refer to sheep in the apostolic writings? Do you know? Five times. He mentions sheep in Matthew 25:31-46 when

He says the sheep will be separated from the goats on judgment day. In John 10:11-15, Christ says He is the good shepherd who will lay down His life for His sheep. In John 10:16, Christ says He has other sheep whom He will eventually add to form one-fold. In John 10:25-30, Christ says His sheep know His voice and they follow Him. And finally, in John 21:15-17, which is His last mention of sheep. The John 21 passage is known as- 'The Petrine Promise'".

Sarah exclaimed, "'The Petrine Promise'?" she asked.

"Yes. Most biblical scholars do not understand it so they have ignored it", Cardinal Romano replied. "But it is at the very heart of everything that the Vatican has been trying to honour through the centuries. Let me explain".

The Petrine Promise

CHAPTER 20: The Promise

The Cardinal sat down and continued with his explanation. "The Vatican knew all about the evidence of Constantine and Caiaphas and Paul's conspiracy. Of course, we knew. But, in our own way, we have been protecting the truth for centuries. We have been waiting for the right moment to reveal the conspiracy and we have never stopped gathering evidence".

Sarah glared at Cardinal Romano. "With all due respect, Your Eminence, I don't believe you. It's easy for you to tell us now that the Vatican was always on the side of right, just when we're about to release evidence of the conspiracy to the world".

The Cardinal looked at Sarah without responding. Then, he glanced down to look at a speck of dust on his trousers. He flicked it away.

"Dr. Chen- I understand that you have an interest in Grigory Kessel's discovery. Is that true? I am sure you are aware that we acquired the Greek Bible manuscript from

St. Catherine's Monastery in the 1950s. Who
do you think provided access to the
ultraviolet light digital scanning equipment
that Mr. Kessel used to make his discovery
of the Syriac undertext? He does not have
access to that type of equipment. Surely, you
know this. We allowed him to use the one in
our Vatican Library. Furthermore, access to
those highly sensitive documents is strictly
monitored. That particular Greek Bible
manuscript is stored in our 'Vatican Secret
Archive'. Permission for access to any
document housed there can only be granted
by His Holiness, the Pope. What does that
tell you, Dr. Chen? The fact that His
Holiness gave his permission for access to
this document with its Syriac undertext-
what does that tell you?"

Sarah was quiet. She couldn't respond.

"Hold on. Just a minute". James was glaring
at Cardinal Romano in disbelief. "Are you
saying that the Vatican knew what was on
that manuscript? They knew that it proved
the Syriac Aramaic text was written before
the Greek text? They knew the Greek New

Testament came after the Aramaic New Testament?"

"Yes, Dr. Bradford. That is exactly what I am saying to all of you. We had already analysed the manuscript. We analyse all of our documents. In fact, Mr. Kessel had expressed an interest in reviewing another manuscript but we told him that his requested document was unavailable. *We* suggested the 1,750-year-old Greek Bible manuscript as a suitable substitute…".

Cardinal Romano looked at each of them in turn, as his words sank in.

The Cardinal smiled sadly. "All along. Through every century. We have been waiting and watching. Protecting. Intervening when we had to. Yes, we even set a trail for Father Thomas to come here. *We led all of you here.* We needed to know, by your reactions, if the world was finally ready for the real truth. You see, the conspiracy didn't end with Constantine at Nicaea. It kept going".

"What?" Sarah, James and Father Thomas all exclaimed in unison.

"It kept going?" James asked.

"Yes. Luther completed Paul's work. Have you not realised that?"

"Luther?" James looked up sharply. "What does the Protestant Reformation have to do with any of this?"

"The Reformation", Sarah's mind raced. "Yes, I see it now- it's when salvation through faith alone became the dominant Protestant doctrine".

"Exactly. The final separation of faith from works, of belief from action. The death of first-century Christianity. It was partly our fault. If we had never abused the practice of granting indulgences, it would not have caused the corruption that followed. Then, perhaps Luther and the Reformation would not have happened…". The Cardinal's eyes had lost some of their fire.

"We tried to protect what little remained of the original message- after Luther's intervention", Cardinal Romano continued. "Luther's '95 Theses' completed what Paul had started. By emphasising 'faith alone,' by completely removing the need for works and accountability, he finished the transformation of Christianity that Rome had set in motion".

"The death of first-century Christianity", Sarah whispered, nodding her head in understanding.

"Look at the historical record", he continued. "When did Christianity begin its dramatic decline? It started with the Reformation's message of easy grace. We in the Catholic Church tried to preserve what we could- the importance of works, of social responsibility. But Luther's message was too appealing to those who wanted salvation without accountability".

"So, the Vatican's been actively concealing the evidence of the conspiracy?" James asked.

"Yes. And waiting. The Church has always helped your Guardians, albeit anonymously, preserve evidence of Christianity's greatest conspiracy". The Cardinal's eyes were tired but clear. "We have been waiting to see if the world was ready for the truth. And I mean the *real* truth- not just about Paul's changes and how the Protestant Reformation took Christianity even further from its origins".

Sarah looked at the scrolls of evidence and then at the Cardinal. "The real truth? What do you mean?"

Cardinal David Romano suddenly looked every day his age.

Sarah's mind swirled. Everything they thought they knew about the Vatican's role and about the nature of the conspiracy itself had changed.

"I will tell you", the Cardinal continued, "if you are ready to hear why we made the choices we made. And learn why modern powers fear Christ's original message even more than ancient Rome did."

"Of course, we're ready ", James muttered quietly, sarcastically to no one in particular. "Bloody ready- excuse my French! I'd really like to understand what the Vatican's been playing at for all these centuries".

"Yes. For you to understand the real truth, there is something I need to explain to you first".

"Cardinal Romano", Sarah interjected, "don't forget that you also have to explain to us what the Petrine Promise is".

The Cardinal looked at her, admiring her quick mind. "Very good, Dr. Chen. I was just coming to that. Do you remember the number **'153'** from John 21:11?"

"Of course", she replied. "Nobody's ever been able to figure out the significance of that number…" her voice trailed off into the silence.

Cardinal David Romano began reciting a passage from memory. His deep, melodious voice filled the room.

> "'So when they had dined, Jesus saith to Simon Peter, **Simon, son of Jonas, lovest thou me more than these?** He saith unto him, Yea, Lord; thou knowest that I love thee. He saith unto him, **Feed my lambs.**

He saith to him again the second time, **Simon, son of Jonas, lovest thou me?** He saith unto him, Yea, Lord; thou knowest that I love thee. He saith unto him, **Feed my sheep.**

He saith unto him the third time, **Simon son of Jonas, lovest thou me?** Peter was grieved because he said unto him the third time, **Lovest thou me?** And he said unto him, Lord, thou knowest all things; thou knowest that I love thee. Jesus saith unto him, **Feed my sheep'''**.

The Cardinal fell silent.

"One command. Five definitions. Three confirmations. **153.** It is the basis of the Petrine Promise". Cardinal Romano said.

"Let me explain. Christ gave *one command* to St. Peter- to look after His sheep. Sheep being the symbol for those who believe in Christ *and act on that belief.* I have already given you the five biblical references to sheep in the apostolic writings. When you study each reference, you realise that Christ used each of these opportunities to define

His sheep - so *five definitions*. Matthew 25:31-46, John 10:11-15, John 10:16, John 10:25-30 and John 21:15-17. And finally, He *confirmed* His command to Peter three times".

Silence filled the room. Finally, the Cardinal said, "There you have it. The explanation of the mystery of 153. Do you understand?"

The three nodded in agreement.

"But there was a problem. A big problem", Cardinal Romano continued. "Do you remember when I said the same forces that feared Christ's message centuries ago fear it more now? I will tell you why.

"To understand their problem, we have to return to the message of the wheat and tares parable. This was always St. Peter's main concern. Christianity was spreading and it was being embraced everywhere. But he feared- if the Church had intervened to remove the non-apostolic writings from the Bible, it might have destroyed everything, just as Christ had warned in the wheat and tares parable. So, he decided to follow Christ's example. Christ had instructed that the wheat and tares should be left in the field, untouched, to grow together. So too, St. Peter instructed that we leave the commissioned and non-commissioned writings together, untouched. The whole 66-book 'Bible' had to be protected and kept together".

As he looked at each one in turn, he said. "Through the centuries, the Vatican has always kept St. Peter's promise to Christ to care for and protect His believers (His sheep). We have honoured 'The Petrine Promise'".

Silence fell on the room once again.

"But David", Father Thomas began. "You're forgetting to mention one very important thing. Christ also said in the parable- in the time of the harvest, the wheat and the tares would be separated. *The harvest is at the end of the world*, according to Matthew 13:39".

"I did not forget Thomas", Cardinal Romano responded. "Let me start by stating what all power structures know- the people they must control can become uncontrollable, ungovernable when they believe that they have nothing left to lose. I am sure you will agree with me that this becomes especially true, if people believe the world is coming to an end".

"Yes, I can understand that. At that point, they will only be concerned with their spiritual destiny", Sarah added.

The Cardinal nodded and continued, "We have all witnessed the bravery that people are capable of *even without these added 'last days' motivations*. Think of the young man who stood against a tank in Tiananmen Square. Think of the Soweto township children in South Africa who stood against apartheid. Think of the Ukrainians today. Human beings are capable of immense courage and resilience when they have nothing left to lose but their sense of self.

"It is this loss of control over people that power structures fear the most; this is their real concern.

"And this became our quandary. As you know, the Church has always depended on donations for its financial survival. The people, corporations and institutions who give us money have always had a vested interest in us delivering a particular type of message."

"It's always about money!" exclaimed James.

"It was a consideration we could not ignore", the Cardinal acknowledged as he continued. "I admit, it was a selfish reason but we had to survive as an institution.

"Anyway, I have now explained to you the reasons why we chose to conceal the evidence. Through the centuries, every Pope has chosen to make the same decision.

"But some time ago, I and others came to believe that continuing to keep the truth of the conspiracy hidden because of a fear of triggering the end of the world or anything else, was no longer the right thing to do. It is time for another way..." Again, his voice trailed off into the silence.

The silence lasted for several minutes. No one moved or said a word; each was deep in their own thoughts.

Finally, Father Thomas broke the silence with a question. "David, did you send the Dead Sea Scroll fragment with the Yair Letter to the British Museum for Dr. Chen to discover so that you could set the revelation of truth in motion?"

"I cannot and will not answer that question, Thomas", Cardinal Romano replied but there was no anger, indignation or even surprise in his voice.

"I have a question", James interjected. "If we decide to release the evidence, will the Vatican back us up?"

"I cannot give you that assurance, Dr. Bradford. You know that I cannot make that decision. I do not have that authority. On my return to the Vatican, I will seek an audience with the Pope. I will update him and await his guidance. But I, personally, will no longer stand in the way. This is the perfect time to return to our most important mission- not protecting the combined message but helping to spread the one true message".

"Before you leave, I also have a question", Sarah said, looking directly at Cardinal David Romano. "The question that Father Thomas just asked you- is that the reason why the Vatican was so organised and prepared for all of this?"

David smiled at her as he answered. "Let me just quote my namesake- was there not a cause? The Vatican had to protect what we could of Christ's original message. We had to preserve some remnant of the truth until the world was ready. We kept all the evidence safe and maintained enough of the original teachings to keep the truth from dying out completely...".

Sarah understood now why the Vatican's resistance had felt different from what she'd expected.

James, Sarah and Father Thomas looked at each other. It had been a shocking few hours since they had arrived in Jerusalem.

The Cardinal stood up to leave. As he did, he looked down at his right arm, which was cradling his worn brown leather-bound notebook to his chest. He said, "Believe it or not, the tradition of this notebook is over four hundred years old. Every one of my predecessors, every successive head of the Vatican Secret Archive, has been presented with a notebook, just like this one, on their first day of office by His Holiness, the Pope. Each of us has used it to record the challenges we faced and the actions we took. And on our deaths, our notebooks have been retrieved and stored together with the Vatican's other classified documents. However, I have decided that on my return to Rome this time, with the Pope's permission, I will retire my notebook and place it with those of my predecessors. I see no further use for it".

As Luca opened the door for the Cardinal to leave, the Cardinal stopped and turned to face them. With his right hand, he held up his notebook for them to see what was written on the front cover.

In worn gold calligraphy, the following words were written- '*THE PETRINE PROMISE*'.

CHAPTER 21: For Such a Time as This

Luca was holding the door open for the Cardinal. He climbed up three steps, hesitated and then stopped and turned around. Cardinal Romano re-entered the room.

The three of them stood up. They were surprised by his return. Luca closed the door and took guard again.

"Dr. Bradford. Dr. Chen. Father Thomas. The decision to continue to hide the conspiracy or, alternatively, to show the world the evidence of the truth now lies in your hands. But, in my opinion, there is just one more thing you need to consider before you make your decisions. And it would be remiss of me if I did not mention it to you".

The three of them looked at each other, bewildered. Cardinal Romano retook his seat. "Everyone, please sit. You need to pay close attention to what I am about to tell you".

Cardinal Romano continued. "In the Vatican Secret Archive, we monitor so many different things. One of the things we monitor is the content of every book, magazine and blog post- in fact, all information released into the public domain every week, in every country and in every language around the world. We have been doing this for centuries. As you may imagine, this job has been made both easier and harder with the advent of the internet. Easier access but more volume". He stopped so that the impact of what he had just told them could sink in. "In this regard, there is only one other Agency in the world that does what we do. I think, all of you know which Agency I am referring to".

He continued. "In 2020, a book was published that you may not have heard of- 'THE APOSTOLIC SCRIPTURES: fundamental Jesus'. It is a compilation of the ten apostolic New Testament Books".

"What?" the three of them exclaimed. "Cardinal Romano- what did you just say?" they asked in unison.

He smiled. "Yes, you heard me correctly. The book- 'The Apostolic Scriptures', with the apostolic testimonies, is already in the public domain. And there is more".

"What?" they exclaimed again.

He continued. "The publication of that book is one of the reasons we decided to assist Grigory Kessel in 2023. But let me not digress. In 2024, the same compiler released a new book titled- LOGOS: the gospel of the kingdom scriptures. That eBook was re-released earlier this year, in 2025, with a new title".

He paused and looked at each of them intently. "Would any of you like to guess what the new title of this book is and what it is about?"

They remained silent and waited for him to continue.

Cardinal Romano continued. "The eBook is now available under the title- 'LOGOS BIBLE: the gospel of the kingdom scriptures'. It is a 49-book compilation of the Old Testament and the Apostolic Scriptures".

He stopped speaking. He could tell by the shocked expressions on their faces that they would need a few minutes to digest this information.

Finally, James responded. "Cardinal Romano- are you telling me that while we have been running all over the world gathering evidence and getting shot at, the 49-book LOGOS Bible is already out in the public domain?"

"Yes. That is exactly what I am telling you".

"So, why hasn't the world reacted?" Sarah asked.

"Because the compiler is not well known. The books were self-published using Amazon. You know how the world works. Her books can be dismissed. Ridiculed. Ignored. But, in the Vatican, we discerned that divine inspiration must have been involved. How else could this unknown have thought to compile these two books?

This realisation brings me to the point that I want you to understand". He paused again.

"Do you remember what Mordecai said to Esther after Haman threatened to exterminate the Jews?"

Father Thomas began to recite the passage from memory.

> **"'Then Mordecai commanded to answer Esther, Think not with thyself that thou shalt escape in the king's house, more than all the Jews. For if thou altogether holdest thy peace at this time, then shall there enlargement and deliverance arise to the Jews from another place; but thou and thy father's house shall be destroyed: and who knoweth whether thou art come to the kingdom for such a time as this?'**

Esther 4:13-14".

"That is correct. Thank you, Father Thomas".

Cardinal Romano looked at them intently. "We did not release the evidence of the conspiracy, when perhaps we should have. So, God inspired this unknown to publish the 'Apostolic Scriptures' and the 'LOGOS Bible'. What is the lesson here? We honoured our Petrine Promise but we missed God's timing". Again, Cardinal Romano paused to give his words a chance to soak in.

"So, this is my warning to you- if you do not release the evidence of the conspiracies, God will find others who *will* carry out His will. That was the lesson Mordecai was teaching Esther. This is the lesson that I am leaving with you today. The purposes of God *will not be thwarted*. For a complete unknown to have published those two books means the Church was late…"

Then, as quietly as he had returned, Cardinal Romano left the room and headed for Rome.

James had been mostly quiet as he had listened to the others talking. But now, as he thought of everything they'd discovered, from the fragment in the British Museum to Constantine's scrolls. It pointed to a conspiracy bigger than they could ever have imagined. Not just a theological cover-up but a deliberate attempt to neutralise the revolutionary power of Christ's original message. And he considered what Cardinal Romano had just told them. They had no other choice. It was time for the truth. They had to make public their findings.

"The world's ready for the truth", James said firmly. "People are hungry for real transformation. Maybe releasing the evidence and causing the removal of non-apostolic writings from the holy scriptures will bring on the end of the world- as the wheat and tares parable teaches us. We don't know. But remember what St. Peter himself said- with the Lord, one day is like a thousand years and a thousand years like one day. We don't know when the end of the world is coming but until it does, we have a responsibility to share the truth with as many people as possible as quickly as possible".

"I agree. The evidence goes public", Sarah continued, "all of it".

Father Thomas smiled. "I was hoping you two would say that. The Guardians have been preparing for this moment for an extraordinarily long time. As we speak, teams are standing by worldwide to share the truth".

CHAPTER 22: Viral

Sarah shook her head as she looked at the table with the ancient evidence of the empire's fear of truth. "They tried to bury Christ's message of justice. They tried to make people forget that faith requires action, that all humans have equal worth and, most importantly, when we act on the side of right, miracles can happen. Ordinary people can accomplish extraordinary things".

"Time to release the truth", James said, moving to a computer station. "Malcolm confirms our teams are standing by to share this evidence on every platform".

Sarah thought of all those throughout history who had tried to expose this truth, who had carefully preserved their testimony for future generations to find.

"Wait". She touched his arm. "One more thing to add". She quickly wrote an introduction to their evidence: "To those seeking truth- what you are about to read proves how Christianity was changed. But more importantly, it shows us what it was

257

meant to be. The message preserved in the LOGOS Bible isn't new- it's the original. It's a call for social justice, for personal accountability and for the transformation of our world. It's the message they tried to hide. It's the message the world needs now. If we act for justice, we have power. Remember JD Greear's famous quote- 'The early church had no building, no money and no political influence. *And they turned the world upside down*'".

James smiled. "Perfect. Ready?"

Sarah nodded, thinking of Caiaphas's words about truth being buried so deeply none would find it. "Ready".

With a keystroke, two thousand years of hidden truth began streaming to the world.

James took her hand. "The truth survived".

"And now it's loose in the world again", Father Thomas said softly. "Just as He promised it would be, in the last days".

The evidence went viral within hours.

***

The three left the facility and checked into a hotel in downtown Jerusalem for some much-needed rest and sustenance.

They had arranged to meet in the hotel's bar, later that evening, for dinner and drinks. When they arrived, all the TV news stations were carrying the same explosive news. Sarah watched the news feeds scroll across the TV screens as people kept flipping through the channels. All the major news outlets were discussing it- BBC, MSNBC, Al Jazeera, CNN, Fox, Bloomberg, Sky News, Wion and more.

Guardian teams around the world were continuing to coordinate the release of every document, every piece of proof they had stored in their facilities.

"We're overwhelming any attempts to suppress it". James commented as he sipped his drink. "Too many copies, too many platforms. The truth is out".

Father Thomas, looking stronger, studied the response data on his laptop. "Look at this-scholars worldwide are already confirming the authenticity of the documents".

Sarah was focused on a separate set of reactions- social media conversations about the LOGOS Bible and its implications.

"People are starting to understand", she said. "Not just the historical conspiracy, but what it means for Christianity today. Listen to these comments:

"'So that's why early Christianity spread so rapidly- it was about real transformation, not just personal salvation.'

'A gospel of justice and accountability makes so much more sense than what churches teach now.'

'This explains everything- why Christianity changed, why churches are dying, why we need to return to the original message...'

"People are ready for the truth". Sarah looked at more responses streaming across their screens. "They're ready to understand what the LOGOS Bible represents- Christ's real message of justice and transformation".

"A message that terrified Caiaphas and Rome", Father Thomas said, "and a message that Luther helped bury even deeper than

Paul had. But yes... its time has finally come".

Sarah's phone buzzed with another update. "The evidence has reached every continent. Scholars, religious leaders, ordinary people-they're all engaging with it. With the truth about the LOGOS Bible and what it represents".

"Nobody can undo this", Sarah said, as she looked at the two men and smiled. "But we need to build on this- something true to Christ's original message. What should we do?"

James was quiet, he didn't immediately reply. "Suddenly, I think I'm in a little bit of shock. I never thought I'd see this day. It's really happening, isn't it?" he said finally. "Everything Caiaphas feared. Everything he tried to prevent".

"No", Sarah corrected gently. "It's everything Christ intended. Everything He said would happen".

Outside, the sun was setting over Jerusalem. Tomorrow would bring a new day, Sarah thought. And for the first time in almost two thousand years, people would be waking up to the truth about what Christianity was meant to be.

The LOGOS Bible wasn't just forty-nine books. It was a revolution waiting to be rediscovered.

CHAPTER 23: The Renaissance

Three months later, Sarah stood at her workstation in the British Museum, watching news feeds scroll across her tablet. The impact of their revelation continued to spread, transforming the understanding of Christianity worldwide.

"The latest analysis just came in", James said, entering the lab with two cups of coffee. Their relationship had deepened since Jerusalem and Sarah still found his half-smile infuriatingly attractive. "Scholars have authenticated every document. Even the critics can't deny the evidence anymore".

"Have you seen the latest survey data?" she showed him her screen. "Church attendance is actually increasing dramatically in congregations that have embraced the LOGOS Bible's message. People are hungry for authentic Christianity".

"A message of social justice, personal accountability, transformation and empowerment", James said, as he set down their coffee cups, "everything Caiaphas feared, everything Luther tried to bury- it's resonating with modern believers".

Her computer chimed with a video call from Father Thomas. The elderly scholar was back at Cambridge, looking fully recovered.

"You'll want to see this", he said without preamble. "Cardinal Romano just made an extraordinary announcement at the Vatican".

Sarah and James quickly switched to YouTube and watched as the Cardinal addressed a packed room filled with reporters from around the globe:

> "For centuries, we tried to preserve what we could of Christ's original message in order to fulfil St. Peter's promise to take care of Christ's believers. But the time for half-measures is past. Today, the Vatican formally acknowledges the authenticity of the LOGOS Bible and the truth about how Christianity was changed...".

"Oh my gosh, it's really happening", Sarah gasped.

Her phone buzzed with more messages and well wishes from around the world. Independent thinkers were embracing Christ's real message. Unchurched believers were finding authentic faith. Communities were forming around the LOGOS Bible's teachings.

"Look at this", James pointed to a particular news item. "'Today, the formerly top-secret society- The Guardians of the Truth, are opening all their archives to share two thousand years of evidence about how Christianity evolved. Universities worldwide are establishing research centres to study the implications'".

"That's so important because..." Sarah's voice was thoughtful, "we can't forget the prophecies about truth being revealed *in the last days*... about the wheat and tares being separated...".

She thought about everything they'd discovered- the conspiracy that changed Christianity, the Vatican's complex role in protecting believers, Luther's final corruption of the message and now this global awakening to the truth.

"Whatever comes next", she said, "at least people finally understand what Christianity was meant to be. What it still can be...".

James touched her shoulder gently. "Ready for phase two?"

She smiled, thinking of their plans to help communities implement the practical lessons from the LOGOS Bible- to show how embracing Christ's message can transform individuals and society.

"The truth is out", she said. "Now the real work begins. Where should we start?"

"Where He started. With a simple message of change. The first thing that Christ said was- 'Change yourself because Judgment Day is coming'", James paused.

"Yes, Matthew 4:17!" Sarah exclaimed.

James continued, "Sarah- a big part of the problem is that our modern world tells you to stay just the way you are. Parents and schools are teaching their children to stay

just the way they are. Friends tell each other-
don't judge me, accept me just the way I am.
But Christ taught us that powerful
transformation is only possible when you
accept that *who you are,* has to change. The
only way to change your community and the
society, is to begin with personal
transformation".

"So, what can we do?"

"I've been thinking about that. In every
community, there are natural leaders. If we
can reach out to them and help them teach
others Christ's true message, then we will
see change- person by person, family by
family, community by community…".

"That's perfect, James. I love that idea. We
do what Christ did and let the transforming
power of His message do the rest".

"Exactly".

"#ChangeChangesEverything. #CCE" Sarah
added with a smile.

Outside her window, London hummed with
life under the autumn sun. Somewhere in
that city, and in cities worldwide, people

were discovering the LOGOS Bible, embracing its call to action, understanding at last what Christianity was always meant to be.

The revolution had begun. Not with violence or force but with truth- a truth that had waited nearly two thousand years to be rediscovered.

And Sarah knew, whatever challenges lay ahead, there would be no going back. Christ's authentic message was loose in the world again.

Just as He had promised it would be- *in the last days*.

EPILOGUE - A New Beginning

The conference hall at Saint Anthony's Monastery was packed. Sarah watched from the podium as attendees from around the world settled into their seats- scholars, religious leaders and social activists, all drawn by the LOGOS Bible's message.

"Hard to believe how much time has passed", James whispered beside her. The desert sunlight streamed through ancient windows. The very chambers where they'd once fled Vatican agents now hosted international gatherings about implementing Christ's authentic teachings.

Father Thomas and Cardinal Romano sat in the front row, an unlikely but powerful partnership in spreading LOGOS theology, the central message of the LOGOS Bible. The Vatican's resources, combined with the Guardians knowledge, had proven instrumental in helping people understand and apply Christ's original message.

Sarah began her presentation: "When we first discovered evidence of how

Christianity was changed, we thought we were just exposing a historical conspiracy. But it's become something much more. People aren't just interested in what happened- they want to know what they can do with their new understanding".

She clicked to her first slide- global data showing how LOGOS Bible-based communities were addressing social justice issues and implementing Christ's teachings about accountability and transformation.

"The question isn't just about what books belong in scripture. It's about what Christianity was meant to be- and what it can still become. A force for genuine change in our world".

As she spoke, she thought about everything they'd discovered since they had released the evidence. Not just the evidence of conspiracy but the proof of how many people throughout history had tried to do the right thing and preserve the truth. The Vatican's complex role. Luther's final betrayal of Christ's message. And now, this worldwide awakening.

She had been receiving messages of well-wishes and encouragement from various LOGOS Bible community groups around the world who knew she was going to be speaking today. People weren't just studying the evidence; they were living His message and transforming their communities using His teachings.

Looking out at the eager faces before her, Sarah felt a profound sense of hope. The truth they'd discovered wasn't just historical fact- it was a living power, changing lives and communities just as it had in the first century.

The revolution Christ had started was finally continuing- just as His prophecies had promised it would- *when the time was right and the world needed His message the most.*

271

AUTHOR'S NOTES

Dr. Celestine is a medical doctor, married and lives in the Caribbean.

'The Petrine Promise' is Dr. Celestine's first work of fiction. She has published three non-fiction theology books- LOGOS Bible: the gospels of the kingdom scriptures, THE APOSTOLIC SCRIPTURES: fundamental Jesus and A CONVERSATION WITH CLAUDE: fresh perspectives on life's biggest problems.

If you have suggestions on how to implement Christ's ideas on personal transformation and community change: **#ChangeChangesEverything**,

Please contact us at: thelogoslifeorg@gmail.com.

Visit our website: https://thelogoslife.org.

273

eBook available from Amazon (https://mybook.to/LOGOSBIBLE)
and Midheaven bookstore (https://midheavens.org).

Paperback book available from Amazon
https://mybook.to/THEAPOSTOLICSCRIP
TURES

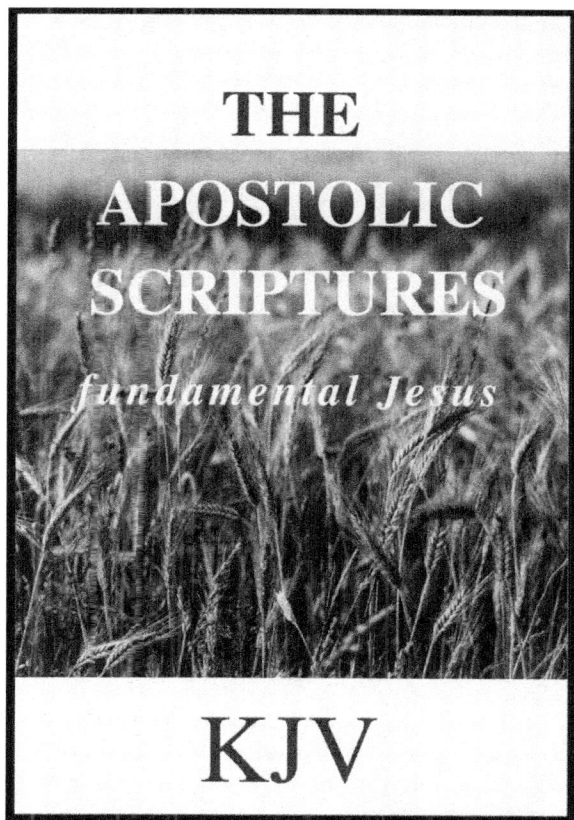

The Petrine Promise

Paperback book available from Amazon
(https://mybook.to/CLAUDEREVISED). eBook available from
Amazon and Midheaven bookstore (https://midheavens.org).

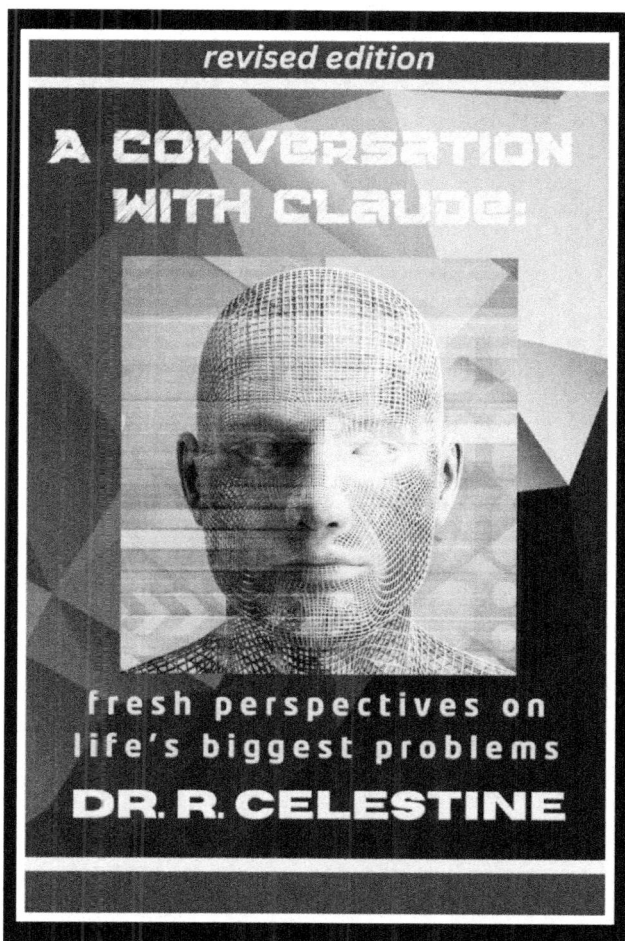

The Petrine Promise

NOTES

NOTES

Printed in Great Britain
by Amazon